A TRILOGY FEATURING:
BOTTLE BABY

WITH ADDITIONAL STORIES...
THREE MONTHS WITH YETI BROWN...
THE HOOTENANNY MASSACRES!

PHILIP W. KUNZ

iUniverse, Inc.
Bloomington

A TRILOGY FEATURING: BOTTLE BABY
with additional stories...Three Months with Yeti
Brown...The Hootenanny Massacres!

iUniverse books may be ordered through booksellers or by contacting:

iUniverse
1663 Liberty Drive
Bloomington, IN 47403
www.iuniverse.com
1-800-Authors (1-800-288-4677)

ISBN: 978-1-4697-9983-4 (sc)
ISBN: 978-1-4697-9982-7 (e)

Printed in the United States of America

iUniverse rev. date: 3/23/2012

Bottle Baby!

FOREWORD

Pre-planned to arrive on time, my entrance into this world was an event precisely calculated by my renowned scientist-father, Doctor-Professor Phillip Ferguson. He is an MIT-alumnus, and a former Pulitzer Prize winner. Dad notified the attending obstetrician, Dr. Christian, that I was on both their day's agenda.

One doctor told the other with certainty that Mom was about to begin her birthing labor as scheduled. Dad drove my mother, Doctor Helen Bowman-Ferguson, a Melon University alumnus and bio-chemical engineer, straight to the hospital that very early morning.

Doctor Ferguson, my soon-to-be father, had determined my scheduled arrival long before Mom's labor pains began. Dad had invented a concoction for Mom, which she simply swished into a glass of purified water, and then drank it to accelerate my delivery in her pregnancy.

Then, in no time at all she was ready to deliver me, almost...except Mother Nature had her own chemistry, also, and both had to agree. Dad had calculated the cooperation and I would come forth on time.

My loving parents had planned everything concerning my birth very meticulously, and premeditated. Phillip and Helen Ferguson had discussed becoming my parents, just as they had contemplated my arrival.

My birth date had to be like clockwork. It would correspond with their vacation schedules. They did not want wasted time, because they were both highly involved people, without much afforded leisure time. It's amusing that they both imagined a child might bring more excitement into their already busy lives. Dad rushed Mom to the Brickfield Hospital at two o'clock to birth me, because babies, they deduced, who were born during early rising hours, were innately smarter.

After a mostly natural-like birthing struggle, admittedly not planned by me, Mom received an unscheduled labor-inducing injection. It tickled me silly. I squirmed uncontrollably in blissful happiness in her water sack, until I could not stay in there any longer. I quickly popped out, in only ten minutes of intense labor, headfirst. The head nurse announced to Mom and Dad that I was born precisely at four o'clock, on that October 31 morn; it was Halloween morning. The world would never be the same.

CHAPTER ONE

When Doctor Christian skillfully held me upside-down and gave me that short flick of his finger swat on my bare behind to start me breathing, I guess he could not have guessed then that he would be the last human on Earth who could physically do that to me. Well anyway, that is how I started my life, upside-down, yelling my lungs out.

After three short days, I grew to know my mother, father, and a kind nurse whom I adored also. Nurse Burns made me laugh with her tickles and funny-face smiles. I liked to laugh. I guess she didn't know it then, but she set the tone of my character for always being happy. She also nicknamed me Philly, short for Phillip.

My busy mother had much to do in her hectic scientific lifestyle. As a consultant to the largest chemical microbiology laboratory on the east coast, she often tested new drugs and anti-virus medicines in her private lab. Her job, considered highly secretive, would not allow Mom to discuss her homework with anyone who was not part of the corporation, not even my father.

She often brought company work home with her, but she never ever showed Dad. Mom's company provided her with a very high salary and she earned every penny. They also provided her with her own bio-contained lab for protection. That part of our home was sealed off, there were no keys. Mom just spoke a complicated memory code into a special receiver that detected only Mom's voice's frequency, which unlocked the facility.

Father was the senior professor in chemistry and the pre-med departmental studies at Cornwell Brown. He often brought home his lecture materials and regularly his own private experiments. He, too, had his own section partitioned off in our large ranch style home, which sprawled out on an Illinois prairie's meadow.

Mom's lab was on the east side, far away from Pop's lab on the west side. In-between, I sat on my blanket learning how to multiply and divide, listening to classical music, while pictures flashed on a big screen TV before me. There was a big smiling pair of lips, from which word sounds were enunciated from a DVD by syllables.

In addition, I was asked to recognize pictures of all the presidents of this country, artists, and just about anything else my parents felt certain that I needed to know in life. I took it all in, long before I could read, walk, or even talk. I just lay there sucking my nutrient-enhanced formula from a bottle and stared amused by all the happenings, especially the flashing lights of the sound mechanisms; all this knowledge, during week one at home. Some babies got a carousel, I got a multi-task programmer computer.

A continuous subliminal melody of facts, figures, and wildlife sounds of jungle shrieks, were constantly inserted into my unconscious mind, played even while I slept. I was supposed to retrieve all this information, which was stored somewhere in my grey matter, later in my life, as I needed it.

Humans only use one tenth of their brain. I guess all the information was to be drawn upon when I entered kindergarten. Some might have thought my parents were child abusers. I thought it was fun.

I had a nanny named Darla with me after Mom went back to her side of the house to do her work. Mom was still close by if Darla needed her, but when she came out from her lab, she had to go through this wash-down ritual and it took a half-hour to get her arms around me to stop me from crying. I cried, only to get to see her when I missed her. However, I missed her a lot.

I loved to greet my loving parents when they "arrived home" after work. After six weeks, no more was I also nursing from my mother's milk. I drank a mixed bottle of scientifically-engineered, human growth hormones and also given a highly-calculated and concentrated, vitamin-enriched formula. Everything I ate, dreamt, or learned was stimulated by my parent's own ideas. The unique ingredients I devoured were always placed in a glass formula bottle, not the ordinary baby bottle.

No, it just couldn't be an ordinary plastic baby's bottle. My parents were convinced plastics emitted toxins, which built up inside our human bodies over one's lifetime to become carcinogens, causing cancers later in life. They simply used the glass test bottles they already had from their scientific experiments.

Unfortunately for me, Dad bought them by the gross with nipples on them to feed his little critters. He had white and gray rats, rabbits occasionally, gerbils, guinea pigs and nutria, and a variety of insects to extrapolate their gene cell stems. It was top science at work at both ends of my house.

In addition, I had another wonderful nanny come to live with us who enjoyed being with me at all times and treated me like her own. Alexis became my surrogate mother, so to speak, after Darla left. Alexis loved to sing to me. She was a college graduate student from Cornwell Brown and had been an assistant to my father. She had majored in biochemistry, but her minor was music. Her grandest wish was someday to perform on the opera stage at Carnegie Hall.

Alexis had a very beautiful face which gave much attribute to her beautiful voice and I loved to listen to her sing me into a deep sleep at naptime. And when I awoke she was still there with her smile.

At only three months, I began to explore our huge home just as soon as I began to crawl. I was expected to perform sooner than most babies did. My knees got sore at first, but just as soon as I became accustomed to those hardwood floors, I realized I could scoot along quickly. My advanced mind told me there was a better way to travel, so one day I just stood up and started walking. My parents were happy with my progress, but unsure if I was too slow to learn. It seemed they kept me on a time schedule as far as baby development and I was lagging behind their expectations.

However, at four months, I had picked up on Alexis's singing and when my mother came to us from her lab workplace one afternoon, mother heard me humming "O Solo Mio" and was very excited and could not wait to tell my father. So she called him immediately upon her cellular and then held it to my mouth. Dad was impressed, but I heard little squeaks in his background and I had my worries about the safety of my dad. Later, I found out he worked with rats...yuck!

CHAPTER TWO

One morning the telephone rang early. It was Alexis calling to tell mother that she was too ill to watch me that morning. Since there wasn't a backup plan, Dad was held responsible for my care, because Mom had important business and Dad always was home in his lab on Tuesdays. Dad was to watch me for the whole day. But he had experiments to complete and he carried me and my highchair into his lab so that I could watch. The lab was full of white rats in cages, with numbers and letters written upon nameplates, to identify their experiment. I could already read it all; I just hadn't tried to speak yet.

Now, I wouldn't tell you that my dad was really an absentminded professor, except that on the only day, which I can ever remember that he watched over me, he was too busy to even remember to feed my formula to me. I was starving.

Dad was busy with his Bunsen burner and doing an unusual experiment upon rats. His potion was a combination of growth hormone/anti-oxidant and a pig pituitary gland mixture, which he was injecting into those little white critters. He hoped his findings would prolong life and initiate a growth spurt in dwarfed people who had been affected by radiation prior to their birth. His heart was in his work, but it was very complicated. I believe it all was directed at problems which had developed after the atomic bomb had been dropped on Japan during World War II.

I sat there watching him nurse each rat from a very small nipple, and then stick them in their butts with a needle. They seemed to like his formula, but not that shot. I could almost hear them say, "More!"

then "Ouch!" as they squeaked from the shot in their behinds. It was like a one-two punch.

I was getting hungrier every minute. Dad was using a liquid mixture that looked just like milk to me, so I decided to take a drink or two of my own when he laid that bottle down close enough for me to grab it. He never even saw me.

And then, while answering the doorbell, Dad picked me up; it was just the newsboy wanting his pay for the month's deliveries, so Dad quickly paid him from his wallet and we hurried back to the rats. They really looked sick to me.

That white liquid was inside a clear glass bottle, which also had a rubber nipple over its top. While Dad got out one of his rats from its cage and examined it, I just reached over and took another big swig or two. It tasted better than my formula to this very hungry kid. It kind of tasted like Mom's cereal which she made for me when she was in a big hurry…yep, just like that!

I did not really feel any affects by consuming Dad's bottle-fed experiment, but those rats sure did! One rat started squeaking loudly, as if in distress. He suddenly began to grow older, right before Dad's eyes, and then rolled over and died. Then that rat just began to shrivel up like a much older rat that had lived out his lifetime. His hair had quickly turned grey, then white, and his tail fell completely off when my Dad picked him up to examine him.

While Dad examined his rat, I took in some more rations and drank that bottle dry. After it was empty and I tried to set it back down, the bottle toppled from my highchair table and hit the floor. When it shattered, I guess Dad then realized he'd set his formula too close to me. After Dad took the time to clean up the mess I'd made, he looked at his watch and noticed it was way past lunchtime.

"Oh, Junior, you must be getting very hungry. Daddy forgot to feed you. I'm sorry. Let's get something to eat," he apologetically spoke.

Dad turned his Bunsen burner off and then the lights in his lab. He pulled me up out of my highchair into his arms and carried me over into the kitchen.

"How's Daddy's little helper doing? You were such a good boy today. Daddy had an important experiment and he forgot to give you something to eat. Now how can we expect you to become that super human that your mother and I hoped you'd become, if I forget to fuel your tank?"

Dad hugged me and I immediately forgave him for being so forgetful. I really liked it when he showed me that he loved me for his son. I hoped he hadn't noticed the white cream that seemed to be running down from the corners of my mouth.

Then he took out one of the many glass bottles from the fridge and warmed it in the micro-wave. He set it for forty seconds and when the sharp tone sounded, he gave it to me. I sucked hard on that bottle, while Dad opened some glassware containers which Mom had left for him to feed me. Each held more special formulated food for my daily intake.

I chowed down and then it was nap time. I suddenly missed Alexis and envisioned her sweet voice singing to me. But during that little nap, I suddenly felt my youthfulness fade and I was having dreams of someday owning a car like my parents' and dating a pretty girl like Alexis.

I guess Pop's formula was already taking effect. I seemed to become so much wiser, but I was still trapped in my small baby's body. My brain was getting much too crowded in there. Maybe that was good, though my thoughts had changed considerably when I awoke; my body was still the same. I quickly realized that I had poo pooed in my diapers.

"Dad!" I suddenly exclaimed. "I soiled my diaper, can you change me?"

I scared myself when I said it, but you should have seen my dad's eyes. He almost choked to death when his soybean-alfalfa-tofu sandwich went down the wrong way. When he hustled over to me, he fell over the ottoman and landed on his keister, right in front of my crib. He managed to get himself up-righted and stared hard at me. His hands grasped my crib's railing as he eased up over my mattress slowly. He was spooky looking, wondering if he was hearing things.

"Eh, what's up, Doc?" I asked him, as he sat there looking dumbfounded, and then really got excited.

"Junior! Junior…eh…did I hear you speak something? Did you just say something, big buddy?" he cautiously spoke out to me.

"Do you smell something? I do-doed in my diapers and it's very uncomfortable. Help me."

It all just came out naturally, as my mind gathered up all the words that I had ever heard in my short life and somehow put them in chronological order to come out that way from me. It was fun. I soon realized how easy the English language was, and Swahili too. Mom had taught me some of that during bath time.

Well, Dad raised straight up, his face white as a sheet, just as though he had seen a ghost. He slowly reached out for me.

"Easy, Pops, don't squeeze me too much, I think I still might not be empty."

Dad jumped back, and then asked me, "Do you understand me when I say you're probably the youngest person to ever master the English language?"

"Sure, it's my parents' fault," I giggled. "They're smart too!"

Dad became all thumbs and danced around like he was walking on tacks. I think he had momentarily lost it, until he got a good whiff of my poopy diaper. Then he came back to reality. All he could say was, "Oh my, oh my, oh my, my, wait till Helen, that's your mother, gets a load of this…she'll lose it."

I guess he thought he had everything under control…yeah, right.

The stinky diaper hit the pail and I was grabbed up by my dad. He took me over to the couch and began quizzing me. Dad asked me all kinds of adult questions; more than I even remember. But one question he wanted to know was if I'd just keep quiet, until he had brought Mom into frenzy with a bet that he could teach me to talk in five minutes. They were always in competition with each other.

That was his plan as he set about getting out volumes of encyclopedias and reading to me as fast as he could. I just let him ramble, because he was having a real good time teaching me.

The front door opened and I could see my mom with bunches of groceries. My dad hustled to assist her and kissed her and asked if she had a good day. Dad seemed so vibrant that Mom got suspicious.

"What's going on, dear? You're acting strangely. Is there something bad that happened while you watched Philly?"

"No, not at all, I had a great day with our son. He's such a smart little guy; takes after his dad, don't you think?"

"Was it his dad who disposed one of the diapers in the kitchen's trash can…then he's got to be smarter than that," she cringed holding her nose, as she grabbed up the trash can and set it out on the back porch. "Those go into the trash, outside!"

"So, how did your trip go at McKinsey Drugs?" Dad questioned Mom.

"They're excited about my newest discovery and think they might go with the compound, if the FDA approves it. I have my name on it, exclusively, and that could bring big dividends for us."

"Gosh, you're always such a surprise. I need some sort of task to get my mental gymnastics going. My rats died again today."

"Did you ever think of using your formula as a rat killer?" she laughed.

"Say, hey, that's quite a great idea! I think you've hit on something. Those rats just sucked that formula down like they couldn't get enough. In ten minutes they were dead…good thinking."

Dad went off into that world of scientists and his brain began to go into overdrive thinking how he could market it, when he looked my way.

"Honey, do you think Philly is smart?"

"He's our son. He couldn't turn out anything but."

"Do you think there is anything to gain if I taught Philly to speak at six months?"

"Yes, you'd waste your time because the youngest person to completely assimilate adult speech was eleven months, three days and that was a hoax on "Believe It Or Not," she advised him.

"I have a theory about the mental transfer of brain waves from one person to another. Like mental telepathy or osmosis through vibrations, we have not discovered yet. I believe if one mind is basically void and empty; the superior mind might install new thoughts into the lesser mind. What do you think?"

"It's been tried before in '72 by Dr. Bausch in Germany. He gave up and settled that Mother Nature had to use her own good old time to develop the child's mind to be useful…although Freud thought it was possible."

"I bet I can have junior talking in say, fifteen minutes, using my secret method that I've been working on."

"Well, I'll make a bet with you for who washes and dries the dishes for a year that though our Philly is certainly going to be very brilliant someday when he grows up, today he'd rather poopy his diapers…right, sweetie?" Mom asked, and then kissed me.

Now, I was confused. I had planned to fool Pop and remain silent until the very last. But not if Mom thought I'd rather just poopy in my drawers, I had to change my plans.

"It's a deal. You prepare supper and I'll take Philly into the living room. I'll be back shortly," Dad told Mom.

Dad picked me up and took me to the living room couch and whispered.

"Philly, can you understand me?"

"Sure, Dad, what's up?"

"Wonderful! Now let's go back and show Mom how well you can speak," he said as he scooped me up and carried me back into the kitchen with a big broad smile upon his face.

"Okay, you think I'm not as smart as you are, right?" Dad accused.

"No, I never said that!"

"But you're thinking it, aren't you?"

"No, but if you continue this line of questioning I might consider it."

"Well, Mrs. Smarty Pants, just listen to this," Dad sounded out to Mom very gleefully.

Mom turned around to watch as Dad closed in on me.

"Philly...what is your name and how old are you?"

Dad turned to Mom, but pointed to me to give her an answer.

"Nah nee blup poo," I babbled out to his bewilderment, while I was laughing hard inside.

"Ha!" Mom laughed, and then asked if that was it.

Mom began to tell Dad how foolish he had been to gamble, hopelessly imprudent, she called him. Dad put his desperate hands upon me and asked me to say something else, anything, just anything.

"Philly, you're my son...answer this for your father, please. Who was the sixteenth president of these United States? Please, you can say it, I heard you. Show Mommy you can...do it for Daddy!"

Dad was getting very upset when I babbled again in baby talk.

"I guess I can finally use nail polish again," Mom began, "since I won't be doing the dishes for a year. Philly, let that be a good lesson from your daddy, never gamble," she warned me.

"Okay, Mom, I'll promise never to gamble," I told her.

Mom became so unstable she almost fainted. Dad had to help her to the living room couch. Mom's head suddenly stuck up looking over the top of the couch at me, wide-eyed and staring.

"Did you really say that, Philly?"

"Sure I did, Mom. Bali we," I repeated it to her, only in Swahili, I think.

Mom's eyes grew large and that was enough to bring her back off the couch and immediately she came to my side.

"Philly, my son…you can really speak? Do you know my name?"

"Sure, it's Mom," I spoke out for her.

"I mean, do you know my given name," she pleaded to test me.

"Well, let's see…it must be Doctor Helen Bowman-Ferguson, just like it reads on your lab's door."

Mom was aghast. She looked at Pop whose smile was now beaming from ear to ear, "He can read too?" they both hollered out in unison.

"Mom, Dad forgot to feed me breakfast today. May I have something more to eat?" I requested.

Mom looked at Dad, who now knew he had opened up a can of worms and looked guilty. Nevertheless, they both realized their prodigy was a genius.

CHAPTER THREE

Things changed quickly around our house then. Dad and Mom brought another person into my life and that was Sugi Agora. Mr. Agora was a local Japanese pianist who taught me voice, along with the piano.

I had watched both Mom and Dad play after dinner sometimes. It seemed down right simple to me. There were just eighty-eight shiny keys on the grand piano and each made its own sound. So, all I had to do was follow the tones, higher or lower. It was just that simple.

My mind told me just to coordinate my fingers with my voice to get the sound out of the piano. When he first saw me, Mr. Agora immediately said to my mom that I was too young to play anything. However, he might be able to teach some simple notes and cords. Nevertheless, he assured Mom it would be wasting his time and her money. Mom said for him to please try anyway and left us alone to begin practice.

When nice Mr. Agora began to try to stretch my fingers upon the keys, he became upset. As I sat next to him, he told me that my hands and fingers were much too short for me ever becoming a pianist. So, while he got back up to summon my mother to complain that it was an impossibility and he was going to resign, I just put my hands upon those ivory keys. I envisioned the way Mom had done it when she played her rendition of Piano Sonata No. 3, by Chopin. It was a cinch because Mom had played it once when she missed Dad!

Mom ran to get a glass of water for poor old Mr. Agora, who collapsed upon the floor when he saw and heard me playing. After he had seen and heard my little concert, he went to speaking frantically in Japanese and neither Mom nor I could understand him. However, he quickly moved to his briefcase and drew out some classical music sheets and placed one before me.

I looked at all those lines and chicken scratches on the pages and somehow my mind coordinated them with my fingers. I just embraced those ivories until Mr. Agora was aghast and fell back into a chair in disbelief of how wonderfully I could perform as I finished up the piece with a little flare.

But, I liked happier music and I hit those keys with everything I had in me and played some honky tonk. Of course, I really did not know what it was, but I had heard it one day on the computer and Dad had quickly turned it off in disgust. But I liked that beat, it was catchy and foot stomping, so that's how I wanted to play.

"Oh…I got a gal ten feet tall, sleeps in the kitchen with her feet in the hall…she ain't nothing but a low down salty dog…ha, ha, ha… salty dog, she ain't nothing but a low down salty dog!" Boy that sizzled! Mom stared suspiciously.

It seems Mr. Agora was impressed, but totally disgusted with me too, for he just up and quit. He only taught refined classical works of the most famous pianists he said as he left. He didn't like honky tonk at all. Suddenly, I had an urge and asked, "Mom, can I borrow the car Saturday night? I want to ask Alexis out for a date."

Mom's eyes bulged and she looked at me strangely. What had I become, she thought? But it was then that she also noticed that my pants were too short and that I was growing; growing smarter; growing bigger; growing some whiskers, too!

Everyday, when I awoke, I was bigger and stronger. In two weeks, I had outgrown my crib and my car safety seat too. Mom and Dad stopped working away from home and spent their entire time with me. I think they thought my body would die from all this overexertion it was going through and they wanted to be near me at the last.

"Phil…the only assumption I can make is that Philly drank some of your rat formula…could that have happened?" Mom demanded.

"Gulp! I hope not. Philly did knock off a formula bottle onto the floor and it broke. He got to it while I was examining my experiments. I don't know how he could have drunk any though. I kept my eye on him constantly."

"That was until he didn't feed me, Mom," I interrupted. "I drank some of that mixture; I thought it was formula like you made for me, Mom. In fact, it was pretty good," I told them.

Mom looked frightened, Dad looked darn right sick. Nevertheless, I felt great. I told them I was bored sitting in my high chair. I wanted a stereo surround-sound chair, also a new Wii X-Box 10000 ultra "Planitaria Maxima" (it had not yet been invented), a big screen plasma TV, and a pool table. Words like that just kept popping out of my mouth all the time. I had learned most of them from watching TV with Alexis. I also told them I had decided on Princeton. That really upset the cart.

My parents quickly sat down and started using their vast knowledge as they systematically began to analyze my predicament.

"Every action has a reaction," Mom began. "What we need to do is formulate your mixture on the scale and attack each sequence of events. Where's your formula?"

"Well, it's among a thousand slips of paper lying on my lab desk. I really hadn't planned on Philly being in my experiment."

"Well, he is now. You and I have to work together on this one. If the word gets out we will both go to jail for child endangerment, much less the health of our child. I am afraid of the consequences. No court will look lightly on this; they'll certainly suspect we put our own son up as a guinea pig."

"Not necessarily, my dearest; not if we help him to become the most superhuman on Earth," Dad suddenly injected with a cynical smile that resembled Dr. Jekyll and Mr. Hyde.

CHAPTER FOUR

It was nice to wake up each morning for those first few weeks and then seeing the smile of my mother. She immediately kissed me and hugged me and then removed my diaper. After I was decent, Mom weighed me on the bathroom scale. I weighed in at forty-one pounds; not bad for a kindergartener or first grader; but I was just seven months old then. I was pushing the yardstick's length and Dad had the kitchen doorway all marked up with my growth-spurt marks from his felt tip pen.

"Whew! He grew almost an inch in November. He's now thirty-six inches tall. Measuring his tibia bone, that relates to being maybe…ah… eight feet tall at seventeen. Gosh!"

Needless to say, Mom bought me a new bed, more clothes and I told her I was definitely through with that diaper. Dad got a Bowflex for Christmas because he felt like he was getting puny and Mom got a treadmill. I got lots of kiddies' toys but wanted a boom box instead.

Mom reluctantly took all those toys back and from then on I made a list of my requests. Only some of them were entirely fulfilled though. Dad refused to get me a subscription to Sports Illustrated so that I could also receive a free "swimsuit edition" calendar. I saw those lovely women in their bikinis and needed that magazine.

I heard a lot of that word "Gosh!" during the next few months. I became a home-taught student by my parents. Mom had received a big subsidy from one of her company-purchased discoveries and we suddenly became very wealthy; well, enough financial support to always have them near me at home.

Alexis had gone and Mom took over being with me, as Dad

frantically searched and searched for the formula but to no avail. He had gone through all of the used up formulas of the day that I might have absorbed some from a bottle.

"I just don't understand it. I've searched everywhere for that chart paper and it's nowhere to be found. It's just a scribbled test equation that I wrote upon a dollar-sized paper. I just can't understand it," poor Dad mumbled to Mom.

"If you don't find it, it will take us years to try and reverse its effects. We must start today going back to square one; I'll help. If and when we do find the exact equation, it might even take years to develop an anti-culture to begin treatment. Keep searching!"

Well, it was really hectic for several weeks, until Dad threw up his arms and finally said that he had just given up. He would search no more and began to design a duplicated new drug and find its cure. Mom and Dad were very busy.

Meanwhile, I was nearly five feet nine inches tall, my hair had changed its color to blonde and I wore a size twelve Nike basketball shoe. While my parents searched for my future, I found a basketball lying in the backyard. I also found out that using my ingenious mind with its great depth perception, determining the angles of shooting that basketball off that backboard was a simple task. Soon it was quick and simple. Swish! Swish! Swish! I quickly became quite the shooter.

Then, I wanted to try to touch the net on the rim. I took ten steps back, ran for the net and jumped up. I crashed into the backboard hard and fell clumsily to the ground. Only my pride was hurt as I dusted myself off.

As I looked up at that goal's rim, it was bent straight up and I had actually touched the top of it. Boy could I jump! I picked that basketball up and stood beneath the rim, jumped up and as I slammed home that dunk, the rim broke off. Dad heard the commotion and looked out to see me on the ground.

"Okay, son, I'm sorry about that old rim. I can see you need a new basketball backboard too. I'll order one from Sears today. You need to romp and run. One day, I'll teach you how to shoot and dribble that thing."

Boy, was he in for a big surprise!

It was one of those afternoon play sessions that I heard voices coming from a yard near ours. Whoever it was, they were having lots of fun and yelling a lot. I peeked over the backyard fence and saw a big park filled with kids that were my size playing games. I watched as one person pitched a ball and another hit it. It was baseball, stupid, I thought. It was just like on TV without a stadium.

I should have told my parents I was leaving the yard, before I left. But I opened the gate to go out and was met by a really bad looking mutt who growled at me. He tried to pee on my foot, so I swung the gate at him and he tumbled into our yard. He was angry, so in self defense, I locked him in our yard and went searching for the laughter. I found it in the ball park.

"Don't just stand there, dopey, grab a bat and hit. Say, are you on our side?"

I had just walked up and I guess the neighborhood kids chose "potluck" because this older girl thought I was on her team.

"I don't know. I just got here."

"Well, we're short a right fielder. Can you play right field?" she asked.

"I don't know. I've never played before," I explained.

Her eyes rolled up and she yelped out, "Why do I always get stuck with the weenies! Get up and swing a bat…you're up," she ordered, pointing at me.

I had seen baseball on TV, while watching with Pop, and he always watched the St. Louis Cardinals play. I liked that number 5 guy, he really smacked that ball. His last name was Pujols. I'd just tell my mind to be like him.

When I stepped up to the plate, the pitcher said I looked goofy.

"Hey, this guy thinks he's Pujols…look how he stands at the plate!"

His team began laughing, especially when I whiffed at the first two thrown pitches. The pitcher was killing me. I think he was in the eighth grade or high school. Anyway, that ball zoomed in pretty fast. I stepped back from home plate and let my mind calculate my swing. Bingo! It told me to hit it hard.

The ball I hit next was the longest ball ever socked over the fence at Brewery Park. The park had been donated by a local beer company and the ballpark had been placed in view of the company on a vacant field. The ballpark was all the way across a four-lane highway, which bordered the left field fence. My ball flew over everything and crashed through a plate-glass window way up on the third floor.

That set off the fire alarm and before it was over, we kids watched over the left field fence as the fire chief came from the building with that ball I had hit. He was holding it in his hand. He looked directly at us, and some kids ran away. But like a dummy, I stood there as he approached.

"Young man, did you see the person that threw this ball through that plate glass window?" he wanted to know.

"Yes, sir, it was I who hit that ball and broke that window."

I could not tell a lie.

"You're not supposed to play ball on that company's lot anymore. That's why they built this park over here, just so you kids could play ball here."

"I was, sir."

"You was where?" he demanded.

"I hit that ball from that home plate over there," I told him, as I pointed to home plate.

The chief looked at home plate, and then swung around as if he were tracking the flight of the ball.

"That's over seven hundred feet. Who are you kidding, son?"

"He really did it!" yelled the little girl who got me to the plate. "He hit that sucker really hard, didn't he? We won the game because of it!" she exclaimed.

The fire chief took off his red fire chief's helmet and scratched his head. Then he looked back at that broken window, then at home plate. He just walked away scratching his head and almost got himself run down by his own fire truck, which carried all his firemen who were headed back to the firehouse.

At first, the fire truck moved forward, and then it came quickly to a halt and backed up. Several of the firemen, and the chief himself, came back to talk to me.

"We've got to see it done. If you really did it with a bat, which is totally out of the realm of possibility, then it's an accident and no charges can be filed. These other firemen called me a loony old goat for believing you. Please, kid, try to hit another one to prove I'm not too old, and should be retired and put out to pasture," he begged of me.

We all walked over to the infield and I picked up a bat. Then I noticed there wasn't a pitcher. The other guys had run away for fear of getting into trouble.

"I need someone to pitch to me, don't I?" I asked the chief.

"Let's see, sure, of course…Jon used to play with the Philly's farm club. Jon, can you throw?" the chief yelled.

A really well built guy walked to the mound and was about to throw even without warming up. I guess he thought it was useless. His first pitch flew back to the backstop and bounced around. Now how could I hit that?

"Here, here, take some of our practice balls," that new girl in my life yelled out from the dugout where there was an equipment closet. She then carried a small canvas bag to the mound. This girl must be the coach, I thought. Not bad on the eyes either…kind of pretty, I thought.

The same girl grabbed a catcher's mitt glove, put on catcher's gear and squatted behind home plate to catch the pitcher. She was really good. Then that fireman became the fire-baller, as his pitches were popping hard in the girl's mitt.

"Okay, big boy, show 'em!" she yelled out.

As I stepped to the plate, I had to know her name.

"Hi…I'm Philly. What's your name?"

"I'm Danielle Strong. Most guys call me Danny. Step in and keep your eye on the ball," she ordered.

For an excellent specimen of the opposite gender, her name didn't do her looks justice.

"Ready?" asked the chief.

"Ready, sir," I said with great uneasiness.

I'm afraid I missed most of the pitches. My timing was off. Therefore, I told Danny I was in big trouble.

"I said keep your eye on the ball!" she reiterated loudly. "You're about to get lucky."

The other firefighters were talking to themselves and the chief was looking mighty stupid, that is, until I finally connected. I almost took the pitcher's head off with a line drive that zoomed straight over the centerfield fence. I got my mind zeroed in on that ball then and after the pitcher got up off the ground, he burned a fastball at me, in spite.

The ball was thrown at eighty-two miles per hour, my mind told me. It wasn't the speed necessary to be in the big leagues, but it didn't matter; my next hit sure was.

The crash of that plate-glass window set off another fire alarm and the chief didn't know if he should hug me or go to his fire alarm call. He rushed to the alarm. The chief was hopping, skipping, and slapping those younger firefighters on their backs and behinds. "The heat is on, boys…let's scramble!" he yelled to them. Those other young firefighters, on the other hand, just stormed away staring at me hard.

"Who was that kid anyway?" I heard one firefighter ask another.

"Nice piece of hitting, Philly. We can use a guy like you on our high school team. Where do you live? What high school do you attend?" Danny questioned.

"Oh, I just moved in," I told her.

"Well, I'd certainly like to see you in a Bulldog's uniform," she said, as she was flirting and looking at me up and down. "My dad's the baseball coach there," she informed me.

I was embarrassed to say the least. Not since Alexis had I had these feelings. Then I heard a familiar voice calling loudly. It was Dad and he sounded disturbed.

"Say, thanks for giving me a chance to play and believing in me. I'll try to come back sometime. Right now, I have to get going, seeya!"

"Bye, seeya around, too," Danny yelled to me as I ran out of the gate.

I ran to the sound of the barking and screaming. It seems my dad and mom believed the pit bull dog that had barged into our backyard and had torn up everything might have devoured me, also. Dad had his pistol, but Mom told him not to shoot just in case that growling dog had me inside of him. They were frantic and had dialed 911.

As I peeked through the fence, I saw my opening. I took about twenty steps backwards and hurled myself over the fence and up into the old maple tree that shaded our backyard.

"Help me down, please!" I told them.

"Well how in the world did you get way up there; and why didn't you answer me when I called?"

Dad was angry and relieved that I was okay, all at once. But I heard that familiar siren sounding and before I could get out of that forked perch, my mom had directed the firemen's double ladder up into the maple tree.

"Say, don't I know you?" asked the chief.

"No, you wouldn't know him, Chief Duncan, he's not been out much," my Dad quickly interrupted and told him to my relief.

I didn't have to lie, and Pop didn't have to know about my home run. The chief just said, "Now I know I'm getting too old! He looks just like that nice kid I met who could be the next Babe Ruth," he mumbled, as he walked back toward his fire truck.

When he turned around to take a second look at me, I smiled and then just gave him a wink to let him know he was really right. He smiled back and then put two and two together. The old chief thought I may be in trouble for the mess in our backyard so he put his finger to his lips to show me he would keep my secret. I liked old Chief Duncan.

A few minutes later, I got another chance to be special. After much ado by the firemen and my parents pondering about that fiercely barking pit bull dog that was still trapped in our backyard and refused to let anyone near him without snarling, I eased over to the gate and opened it.

The pit bull charged over to me, but stopped short of Dad shooting him when he got too close to shoot. Dad had the water hose aimed directly at him. The big mutt stopped, and then licked my bare leg very affectionately. He wasn't mean at all, just cranky, because of me locking him inside there. Then he waddled out of the gate, wagging his stubby tail all the way down the street.

We all watched as that dog meandered slowly into a nearby yard, left his scent right at the entrance to let other dogs know that land was his alone, and then hopped upon the doorstep of our new neighbor. The dog barked several deep, off-key howls, and then pawed at the front door. When the door finally opened, I heard our new neighbor's son ask him where he had been. The boy bent down to hug his returning friend and got a big sloppy lick. He hugged him repeatedly as the dog jumped up again to lick his face. Then the boy patted him on his head, before the pooch strolled gallantly inside as if he owned the joint.

I guess the mutt was checking out his new neighborhood. He needed a leash to be outside, or the pooch would get to visit the city dog pound, Dad assured us very angrily. I never saw him so upset as then. Dad hoped the owner would be fined for allowing his dog to run loose. I thought he was overly tough on that pup. I think I would have liked to have had him as mine. I planned to ask my parents for a pet. Maybe, I could get a dog like the one my neighbors had.

That day was a big learning day. I realized the pain my parents felt from my not telling them I was going walk-about. They decided to ground me for a week. However, because Mom said they hadn't told me not to go out on my own, they scrubbed the penalty and gave me lots of hugs. I also learned how nice it was to be with other kids and have them compliment me, especially my hitting. It was a good day.

CHAPTER FIVE

Mom and Dad became my companions. We spent every day and sometimes nights together for weeks, until they decided their knowledge was limiting my thinking. Then they bought a huge new megabyte computer that allowed me to ask questions of those which Mom and Dad did not know the answers.

It's fun to learn and I was really having a great time, but after a long while I felt my fingers getting sore and my eyes very tired. It was time for a family break. We all agreed a vacation to Disney World would be educational and relaxing. Several days after planning and packing, we all went to the airport.

Flying aboard a jet passenger plane was intriguing. All the way to Orlando, Florida, Mom was telling me to be certain to notice all the different cultures of people who would be walking around having fun, too. It was proof, she said, many cultures could co-exist on our planet and live peaceably together, if only they tried.

On the other hand, Dad wanted to make me aware that some people carried diseases they might not even realize they conveyed and I should watch out for those, whoever they may be. I thought he might be spending just too much time with his white rats.

My vacation didn't start, of course, until we landed at Orlando International Airport and then our driver taxied up to our hotel. It was all fascinating and exciting, especially when I got my first look at Disney World from our hotel room. It was amazing; just as I imagined.

Now mind you, I had actually been pre-schooled about Disney World. One of the DVDs I had watched was concerning fantasy versus reality. Fantasy was what one's mind envisions; reality is what really existed. I suppose Disney World was both. It ran past my mind during my mental subliminal indoctrination period, and I now recalled everything in my mind.

I wanted to head for the roller coasters. I didn't need the park's map. The park's map also was inserted into my mind. Then it happened. I saw Mickey, Goofy, and Tinker Bell walk into a secret door behind our hotel, the Polynesian Resort.

I quickly took Mom by the hand, while she was holding Dad's. I litterly dragged them both through and around crowds, until we stood before the characters, as they welcomed us to Disney World. Dad was shaken by my strength to pull them both. Mom was already sore from being yanked around.

I watched as the other kids who gathered around had their pictures taken with the three Disney World stars. My mind was on that fast moving, monster rollercoaster which opened at ten. That was the exact time it opened. To my surprise, Mickey's squeaky voice told us all to get onto the overhead rail train to be first into the park. Everyone ran to fill the train's seats, but I held Mom and Dad back.

"Son, we have to get on the train or we'll miss the opportunity to be first into the park."

"Dad, hang in there. When it's loaded, we'll jump on last. That way, we'll be first off the train," I told him.

"Amazing," Mom told me.

"Then let's go now," I spoke, as I again dragged them to the last unfilled car. My mind had told me that the Disney stars got on last and when the door of that train had just about shut, in popped Mickey, Tinker Bell and Goofy. Guess who sat right next to me, as she always did in the DVD? Yes, it was Tinker Bell and she was so pretty, too.

Our door opened first as the Disney stars got out to lead the happy vacationers into the park. Goofy grabbed my hand and we skipped together on down the road to where he turned and said good-bye to us all.

I didn't waste time with Dad on one arm and Mom on the other. I headed to the Big Mountain roller coaster. We were first in line, but I got a bigger surprise.

"I'm sorry, young man. You must have a partner and he or she must be forty-eight inches tall to get on this ride," he nicely told me.

I looked over at the "how tall you must be to ride this ride" sign. Most of the kids wanting to get on the ride stood a bit too short, and they sure looked sad.

"How old are you?" I asked a boy with a St. Louis Cardinal's ball cap on.

"I'm twelve, but I'm short for my age and that fellow won't let me get on. We came all the way from Springfield, Illinois and I can't even ride the best ride in the park," he sighed.

"Come with me and stand tall," I decreed.

I had the answer, when I told the ride attendant to look at the boy standing next to the how tall sign. He was now over forty-eight inches. I had simply pushed that sign into the ground with my hands behind my back and it sunk in about four inches. He then reluctantly said okay, but scratched his head in disbelief.

While he was examining the sign, we all ran to get onto the roller coaster and then off we went. That ride was very slow at first. It crawled up and up slowly on its tracks to the top. Then, whoosh! We all came down in a mad freefall, at a speed I calculated in my brain as sixty-seven miles an hour. Before we could recover, we zoomed up and over, upside-down and around so fast, Mom began screaming bloody murder. I told her to just let it all out, because that next crash dive was a real doosey.

I heard more loud screaming sounding out above everyone else's. Then I noticed it was Dad who was yelling so loud, not Mom. Now that was a bit embarrassing, but nobody except me noticed how glad he was to get off when we stopped. It was terrific.

"Once is enough, son," Dad quickly told me and my new friend Galen, when we jumped back into a "get-on" line. Before Dad knew it, he was on, too, with Mom and he was screaming bloody murder again. This time Mom took his picture. What an awful face he got caught making! I thought I'd better let Dad off the hook on a third trip, because he appeared a bit green around the gills when we all sat down on a bench. My new friend thanked me and away he went to another ride.

After I had a quick sip from Mom's ice water, we headed to the next big attraction and that was Buzz Lightyear's Space Ranger Spin. Now I snuck in that one, too, but I was the one feeling a bit queasy getting off. That spin's centrifugal force pinned me back against a wall so hard,

I almost slipped through the cracks. Luckily, I was strong and getting stronger by the minute. It seemed as if the activities were causing my body to grow and soon my shorts and shoes felt tighter.

"Phillip! Philly looks strange. Do you feel all right, Philly?" Mom asked.

"I think I'm growing, Mom. My mind tells me it's the result of my dendrites being lit up by the excitement, overcharged by the kinetic energy into my pituitary. My pituitary is sending messages to all of my body parts to expedite. Do you see the hair now growing under my pits? Maybe we should just settle for a boat ride through the jungle," I suggested.

The African Jungle Cruise was cooling and I felt better. That is, until I whacked a big ten-ton hippo that came up from under the water and scared us all. When I noticed the stunned look upon our tour guide's face when I shattered that thing with a right hook, she stopped speaking and just stared wide-eyed at me. I think she was doubting what I had done, but so was Dad. He didn't want to have to pay for all that damage.

I restrained myself when gators' jaws opened wide and a close-charging water buffalo brought a rise from the people aboard. Boy, did I get a close look when I exited on the plank going off the boat and back into the main park. Others started pointing their fingers my way.

But it wasn't until my dad had to buy me a costume of a super hero, because it was my new bigger size that made everyone worry, including me. I broke the door latch off the dressing room by accident just turning the handle. Nevertheless, my super strength forthcoming, was not too soon.

I guess it looked weird for a guy my new size, almost six feet tall, holding my mother's hand. Both Mom and Dad stared at me as if I was still growing. Looking as if my clothes were going to explode off my body, we all decided to hurriedly go back to our hotel.

Suddenly, everyone heard screams coming from Dumbo's flying elephant ride. A mother who wasn't supposed to hold her child without her restraint on, did. The four year old child had leaped out of her arms and luckily was hooked by Dumbo's curved trunk. If the ride operator had suddenly stopped the ride, she might have fallen off or have been crushed by another elephant. He was frantic as to what he could do.

My mind went into super-speed and I saw a way to rescue the girl on her next time around. When I let go of my parents, I leaped on top of that elephant at its lowest point and scooped up the child before it again rose up high into the air. I then jumped off with the child held closely in my arms as we both fell onto a tent's top, just like a fireman's net. She clung close to me as we slid safely off the tent, onto the ground. I had brought her down safely. I learned the girl was named Kellie.

When the ride stopped, everyone came running to us applauding my courage, except my dad, he just fainted. Mom sat beside Dad upon a bench, fanning him.

"Who is that superhero?" came voices yelling out from the crowd. My new shirt only had a big letter B imprinted on my chest, but attached to the shoulders was a cape. I guess I looked the part, but no one there knew of any superhero's whoever looked like me.

Then the mother of the child came screaming while running to us. She fell to her knees and hugged her daughter, then rose up to me, holding little Kellie in her arms. The mother was crying happy tears, but then she actually kissed me. That's just when someone took their cell phone out and caught the occasion and sent it to the media.

Anyway, that was the scene on the nightly news. It was all about an unknown hero, who was dressed in leotards with a cape and the letter B on his chest. It was he who had rescued a little damsel in distress. I was seen nation-wide.

We had to leave the park, because the security asked my family and me to meet the people in charge. They also wished to thank me and did so with handshakes and thank yous. They told me they wanted to grant any single wish for me personally. I thought about it just one second. I realized my hearing had also become acute while on that wild ride. I heard something I thought was a bolt snap, but I wasn't certain. I wanted to find it.

"If I could, I'd sure like to ride that roller coaster just once more, but alone. Maybe for one solid hour, if that's possible."

Now they thought I was a bit unselfish, not to request money or a lifetime pass.

"When I rode that roller coaster the first time, I noticed a blip or pop at one of the bottom-outs. I'd like to recheck it, because it bothers me to think there might be a mishap there."

"There can't be. Our inspection crew diligently goes over every inch, every single day it's in operation. Nevertheless, if that's your wish, so be it, and thank you again. Presently, it's a bit too crowded right now, but will you and your parents join Mickey and friends for breakfast? Where are you staying?" he asked Mom.

"The Polynesian," she replied.

"Then tomorrow morning it is…two hours before the park opens, you'll be on that ride…until then," the gentleman told me.

We were whisked away by golf carts to the Polynesian, where Dad crashed upon his bed. It was just too much for him.

We watched one account on TV of the heroic rescue at the park and of the reward of her kiss. The interview of the parent was apologetic. She admittedly put her child on her lap, after being told not to. She thanked me over the air again and the interviewer said my name on national TV. Mom was beaming, Dad was snoring. He really, really needed rest from his work, Mom said.

Then, Mom and I sat down, because I had something I thought was important to their unmanageable experiment and my life depended upon it.

"Mom, I realize this vacation was for us to spend some time together; maybe our last days together. I can tell by your touches that you feel I might expire before you can discover a reversible plan of my demise. That's why I thought of that long roller coaster ride in the morning. The exhilaration, the thrill of being on that ride caused me to really sprout up.

"My mind is set for being an adult. I think it is necessary to know if my body will keep up. Will I grow into a giant, a tall basketball player, or will Mother Nature step in to curtail this happening and return me to being normal at the end? I'm not afraid, Mom, and I hope you and Dad won't be either.

"I have lived only a few months, but really I have the world's knowledge of a very old, learned, scholarly person. I'm banking on this experiment in the morning. All I ask is you and Dad understand I want this to take place this way. Therefore, if something goes wrong, I did it my way, okay?"

"You may be correct, Philly. Your father is tormented and I don't know how he will handle this if something goes wrong. You certainly proved he was on the right track in his experiments and sometimes scientists must sacrifice themselves for the good of mankind. I suppose you know what you are doing better than your father and me. I'll be there beside you to see you through…"

"I'll be there, also, son," Dad broke in to tell me from his bed. He had heard the whole idea, got up and hugged me.

"If we're all going through with this experiment together, we all had better try to rest. My immediate calculations are that I am six feet three. Therefore, a future generation normally grows approximately three inches taller than the parents…ah, their father. You, my son, should have attained a six feet six height at the time of your adulthood. Accordingly, we best find clothes for you before you go on that ride, if that growth spurt reoccurs."

"That's precisely what I thought, Dad. Let's sleep on it."

Morning would not come too soon. I was up at daylight and stood looking out our room's window over the park's grounds. I spotted that big rollercoaster and that excited me just thinking about how I would get the chance. I was a bit nervous, but I had no choice that I could see that was better. Do it and get it over with, good or bad.

There were only the seven of us as we sat down early for breakfast with the cartoon characters and the park manager. It was special, because Tinker Bell sat beside me. I suppose even though my mind was of an adult, there's always that kid inside of us.

Quietly, right after the meal, we all casually strolled out to several electric carts, got aboard, and then headed out to that big rollercoaster. I didn't know it, but Dad had to sign an injury release of the park and its manager. Dad was to be solely responsible for anything bad that might happen to me by being alone on the ride.

Dad had also asked privately, if the park's costume department might have an unused superhero suit that I might wear for the event. They told Dad they contemplated many different superheroes before, but could not find one that would not infringe against someone's superhero copyright.

Then Dad let the cat out of the bag about my growing plight. After those people heard of my intriguing situation, they all decided to help me, just in case it was my last. Checking with their costume department it was told it could be done in minutes. They are the most generous people, always.

Dad immediately came up with a new superhero name out of necessity. He announced that I, Philly Ferguson, was now officially the first named "Bottle Baby" hero. The costume people already had the red Bs, the purple cape and the green shirt and laced boots. I would be set to debut.

We stopped outside their costume department. A man took me inside where I was quickly fitted to a cape and suit in only moments from their vast assortment. Two big Bs were quickly ironed upon the chest. And when I slipped into that spandex, I felt super, too.

Bottle Baby flies through the Arch

To my complete surprise, as I walked out wearing the costume, I was met by the media. They were invited by the manager to view my requested rollercoaster event. I only posed one time, then I was whisked away up to the Big Mountain rollercoaster.

Up the ramp I walked to the first car of that rollercoaster. I was led to the car and then buckled in tightly. A safety bar, which I was told to hold on to, was pulled down before me. That held me securely.

As I was seated inside the car safely, I couldn't help thinking how these safety devices were designed to keep me safe and that little Kellie's loving mother had foolishly placed her little girl in harm's way by not obeying the park rules.

"Good luck, Philly. Enjoy your ride," said the park manager. "If you decide you've had enough, just put up one finger and we'll stop you right back here…let'er go!" the man yelled to the control room operator.

The cars began their crawl forward and I felt the excitement mounting, when I headed straight up pointing to the clear blue sky.

As I rose to the top of the very first rise, I looked down and saw Mother and Father standing below waving. There were TV cameras pointed at me and an applause began. And then that sudden rush of adrenaline came as the freefall downward began…the race was on.

I didn't hear that funny sounding blip that I first heard on my last ride. The speed was faster and a bit bumpier than I expected. My mind told me it was a result of being much lighter. It also told me I had better hold on as the cars whizzed up and over and around. I waved to everyone on my first pass, but the cars didn't stop. Again and again, I felt the pull of Gs and the centrifugal forces pulling sideways upon my body.

I began to feel the movement in my body and the strength I was building. Each pass made me stronger and stronger, until I was bursting inside with pent up power.

Each time I went over a quick rise and fall, I felt as if I could fly. My mind generated the facts that air is matter, occupies space and has weight, just as water does; only the density of water was greater than air. I might be able to swim in the air if I was fast enough. Nevertheless, like a bird flapping its wings, if I could generate enough speed by flapping my arms, just like a hummingbird does, I, too, could go airborne.

My energy rose to unbearable heights and I was bursting at the seams. Either I was going to put up that one finger to stop, or take that next step in the life of Bottle Baby, super hero. I decided the latter.

I tested my wings by extending my arms. I found I could then flutter them so fast that they couldn't be seen by the human eye. And even though I was in full force Gs going downward, I almost stopped the speed of the whole rollercoaster by flapping. I had super liftoff powers.

"Let's do it!" I hollered out on the next pass to Mom and Dad. They hadn't the slightest idea what their son was about to do next.

I think it was on pass forty-one that I could sit still no longer. When I discovered my seat belt wouldn't budge, nor that safety bar either, I waited until I had reached a far pinnacle and exploded from the seat into the air.

It took a moment for me to realize I could jump just so high. I was enjoying my freedom up high in the sky. But when I saw the faces of the ant-like people showing clearer, I knew I had better begin my flutter. Gravity was pulling me down to Earth.

I was slowing quickly, as I got almost to the ground and reversed direction and streaked back up into the sky like a missile. I was higher than a jet in only moments and felt the lack of oxygen content in my breathing, my being up over ten thousand feet into the stratosphere.

A cameraman, who had captured the whole event from the beginning, said he didn't know where I had vanished to so quickly. He was rapidly putting his segments into the park's big TV teletron screens for everyone to view. Mom held Dad tightly, thinking that was the last time they would see their son.

I, on the other hand, realized that I needed lots of practice and some sort of directional control. While zooming over the Gulf of Mexico, I pivoted my left foot and I zoomed off to the right. "Right is left and left is right!" I told myself to remember.

My energy was still as high as it was when I had begun and it seemed never-ending and untiring to flutter. I spotted a speck of white out in the Caribbean, so I eased up to see what it was. I soon became aware of a derelict boat drifting out in the deep. I thought I might just perch there for awhile and enjoy being out on the sea.

I planned to light on the deck of that boat. I missed my mark almost twenty feet off the stern of the craft, and splashed down into the sea. That was a good learning experience, because if I had hit that boat, it would have sunk. Salt water, denser than freshwater, caused me to abruptly return to the surface like a cork. When I surfaced, I was face to face with a very confused and helpless family of five, whose boat had become stranded without power. Their powerless craft was drifting at the mercy of the sea currants, which unfortunately weren't taking them anywhere towards shore or being rescued.

I swam for the first time in my life, because I was still fluttering. I learned to halt all of my body movements using "mind over matter", so to speak. I reached up and was pulled aboard by a bewildered looking man, who was armed with a gun.

"Hello, I'm Philly Ferguson. Can I help you?" I first asked.

The man fainted in my arms and his gun fell onto the boat deck. I picked it up and saw it was empty. The wife came to me and was very weak. In Spanish, she told me that they were starving and hadn't eaten for over a week. They had been derelict for three weeks and had put in at Port au Prince east of Jamaica. I had to help these poor stranded souls.

Since the sun rises in the east, everywhere in the world except the Artic and Antarctica, my mind told me by their drifting figures, the closest land would be Jamaica. However, I decided the longer trip back was more sensible. I told them I would try to help them.

I peered off into the vast unlimited easterly direction. My mind calculated a boat traveling one hundred miles per hour could make the trip back to Port au Prince in four hours. I picked up the man and asked them all to lie to the rear of the craft to raise the front end, so the bow would cut more easily through the waves. I explained to them in Spanish that I was going to pull their boat, at a very fast pace and if they threw off all the excess baggage, it would certainly help.

The children ran around like little mice and threw over the deck chairs and whatever wasn't nailed down. I broke off the anchor and grabbed the tie down rope.

"Bueno…vamanos!" I told them, when everything was overboard. It was good to use a language I had only learned in my sleep. I was a bit proud of myself when they all easily understood me.

As they all sat up against the stern's wall, I began to flutter. The boat began to follow. It took about five minutes to get that craft skimming the water at about one-hundred-ten. Luckily, the fiberglass was built to take it and the sea was calm. I looked back and felt good inside to see the people with smiling faces.

In less than four hours, I spotted Port au Prince. I then eased up my fluttering, until I found myself dragging the boat up onto a beautiful, white sandy beach. Before I could let go of the tow rope, everyone had leaped off the boat and headed to the coconut palms, which held their next meal. They were desperate. Those castaways started telling everyone how I saved their lives and I felt a bit crowded. When a crowd began to assemble as did the policia, I just fluttered away in a second, back out to sea.

When I looked back, hundreds were astonishingly waving to me. Another deed for humanity, I thought. I felt even more power inside of me for doing good, and decided to take it to the limits. I didn't hear the sonic boom, of course, but I knew I had broken the sound barrier. Then, I ran into a problem.

I headed back to Orlando and our hotel at speeds my mind told me were incalculable. That was because there were no reflectors, such as trees, which could return signals to register on my mind when they bounced off frequencies like radar does, whatever that was…I thought of lasers.

When I found myself dangling my left foot, which caused air friction and thusly some wind drag, it caused me to veer off above the Atlantic Ocean, instead of the gulf. I knew I was headed in the wrong direction when I crossed over the Bahamas, ninety miles east of coastal Florida. I suppose it was my fortune, for when turning west, I witnessed the USA's space shuttle, Atlantis, zooming up from its launch pad at Cape Kennedy.

When the huge spaceship zoomed past me, I took a deep breath and tailed it up above ten thousand feet. Quickly, I was met by several unfriendly fighter jets that eased up beside me to see if I was a danger. They were our government's interceptors.

When my body recognized I was being zeroed in upon by one pilot's laser tracking beam, I feared I had better skedaddle. I think they had thought I was a missile as I abruptly achieved super sonic speed to avoid that little fiery lighted match that had me as its target.

They had actually fired upon me. I zigged, then zagged, up and down and around, just like that rollercoaster, until the trailing exhaust of that missile's rocket smoke spelled out USA, USA…help!

Next, I took a deep breath and zoomed straight up into the stratosphere, higher than I had been before. The missile expired and fell back into the ocean. I glided across Florida, until I saw that big geometric silver sphere on the park's property and landed on top of it.

With one last burst, I landed outside the Polynesian Resort in their beautiful lake and stayed there resting from my near death encounter with the US government. After dark, I went up to my parents' room and knocked. Dad stood there in disbelief and Mother in shock, then they launched to me and grabbed me and hugged me crying.

"We thought you were dead, but there was no proof," Dad said. "Poof! What happened? How are you feeling now, son?"

Dad would not release his hold upon me nor Mother, as they dragged me to their bed to sit next to me. I realized I was a bit taller than they were and my suit was getting too small.

"First, I feel very, very well, thank you. I discovered you're a genius, Pop. Because of your secret formula, I have many powers. I'm strong, how strong I haven't been tested as yet…I can hear very well. Remember that blip I heard during that first rollercoaster ride? I discovered that it was simply that someone had opened their mouth, probably screaming bloody murder, and their gum fell out and stuck onto the track. It dissipated quickly with each passing wheel. Were you chewing gum then, Dad?"

Dad looked embarrassed. Mom looked at me and was about to laugh.

"Anyway, the best of all is I can fly…I can fly very, very fast. So far, I've just been to the Caribbean. I flew up along side the space shuttle over the Atlantic, just an hour ago, and I learned that I can zoom anywhere I want, or wherever I am needed.

"Mom, I think I need your help to make my suit fit better. Maybe it should be made of micro fiber, or something to help in air drag. Dad, got any more ingenious ideas?"

Then to prove my flying ability, I leaped off the balcony, zoomed around over the park, and came back to light upon the balcony to Mom and Dad's delight.

"Hey, I think I'll take some of my own experiment juice!" Dad said excitedly.

"Let's get back to our labs and create a new suit for our hero!" Mom squealed out.

We soon checked out and I was wearing one of Dad's suits. As I peered out the return jet's window, I knew someday soon I would return to see the rest of that wonderful amusement park.

CHAPTER SIX

There's no place like home, except now I had only infant's clothes to sleep in waiting for me, not any adult sized. The only words spoken by Mom and Dad when we arrived were, "Oh my!" My new child's bed was too short, also.

To be comfortable, that night I slept in Dad's pajamas and on the family room's couch. I watched the "Up to the Minute News" and heard their numerous reports of a strange celestial person flying down from the sky in Florida. I was observed flying next to our spaceship Atlantis, too, and there was a picture of me to boot. I looked pretty spiffy! But they didn't show a facial shot, so who would have known it was I who dawned that cape in the name of honor and justice?

Word was received that this space invader had visited Central America, also, and was a peace-loving humanoid type. I fell asleep dreaming of all the good I could do with my new powers. If I only had limited time in this world, I wanted to leave a good mark on my report card. Mom had other ideas.

"Son, your mother thinks you should now enroll in a private school that will test your abilities and then grant you learned experience for your knowledge. Everyone needs a good education and we have done our best. But we can't give you that diploma that proves you are an educated person."

"Okay, Dad, but if Mom wants my opinion, it's if you send a fool to college, all you get is an educated fool. Therefore, it's not how brilliant one is then, it's because he paid his college fees that got that sheep skin. There are lots of geniuses walking around without a college degree.

It's who you are, who you want to be in life and how hard you are willing to work at it that establishes your expertise and future, barring accidentally drinking your dad's experiment, that is."

"Gee, sorry again, you might have something there, son. But regardless, if your powers someday fade and you return to a normal being, you'll need that sheep skin degree," Dad wisely advised.

So, I eventually took the ACT, PSAT and the mammoth entrance exams for Notre Dame University, several weeks later. That was the largest private college Mom knew. After much ado over my successful testing, their scholars placed me in a class of my own...that is, they simply asked me to teach, teach everything or anything that I wanted; after I had aced their four thousand question exam. Mom and Dad were thrilled by their own diligent teaching process and especially my retention span.

Bestowed upon me was a degree of "highest learning". It was a new achievement in the world order of teaching. I was to become the Professor of Everything.

Somehow, the very thought of standing before several hundred great students, all themselves from a highly-selected group; I chose to become their librarian temp.

I wanted first to see just how college life affected my thinking. I was also asked to enroll and complete my general studies courses... then my BS.MB.PHD.MD.DDJP. degrees would be actually earned. In addition, I would write a thesis in my fields, whatever they would turn out to be. Two days later, after I had completed the task at super human speeds, I graduated cum laude, twenty times. A feat that still stands unblemished today.

All the kind faculty professors came to me to discuss their new ideas in teaching and received my learned thoughts and suggestions. But I demanded that each make their own decisions. It was working out quite nicely, until the head football coach thought he could get a leg up on his opponents, if I could just sit up in the press box and call out the next play for his team. I did just that one Saturday next, while being broadcasted on TV. We were losing badly when the coach addressed me over the headset that I was a failure.

"The only help we need now is the guy upstairs and I don't think he's worried about football these days."

I realized I knew nothing about football and there wasn't time to learn any plays right then with just one quarter to go, and losing 21-0. But, if possible, I thought of how I could contribute.

"Coach, is there an NCAA rule that prohibits a new student, not on scholarship to play?"

"Now what, genius?"

"I'd like to play…right now!"

With my super human speed, I flew from the press box way up high, down through that hallowed tunnel and into the locker room. The only uniform not in use was a tattered practice jersey with the number "0" on its front. I put it on, grabbed a helmet and before coach could answer, I tapped him on the shoulder.

"What the…?" the coach yelled when he saw me behind him.

"Put me in coach…I'm ready to play," I told him. "I must be the middle linebacker."

"I can't take our star defensive player out!" he fumed.

"It's 21-0…you'll have to trust me."

"Get in zero…number fifty-five, you're out!" he yelled.

I appeared inside the huddle so fast, the ref walked over to see if we had eleven players. There I was.

"Fellas…I'm your new middleman…coach sent me in…what's your favorite play called?"

They knew me, but I was met with some opposition, until finally we went back into our defensive huddle. The huge, knowledgeable, defensive tackle spoke, "Red bone right, double flex, ultra, 62 bleep!" he hurriedly called out.

"Okay, fellas…that's the call now, but instead of blocking anyone, stand up and be still, because here comes our first TD," I said looking across at the opposition.

The snap was good, however none of my guys could help but use their talents and forced a pass. Using my super human speed, I went back on what was a certain touchdown pass and intercepted the football. I returned the ball so quickly, all anyone saw was me standing in the end zone with our first TD.

The refs conferred and reviewed the replay, because they thought it was a trick play. Even in slow playback, I was too fast to identify, until I stopped in the end zone. Their arms went up after further review and I was able to repeat that three more times to win the game. However, I wasn't available for interviews after the game. The TV focused in on that empty number "0" jersey thrown down on the locker room floor. I was out of there.

My playing days were over. I missed Mom, so I tendered my resignation and left that great college. My thinking was I needed to help humanity more and a motherly hug was awfully nice when I got up each morning and before being tucked into my bed. After all, I wasn't one year old yet. Nevertheless, I was ready for my world.

I sat down and began to think about how I could disguise my identity so that no one would rush to me if I did something good. I didn't really care for publicity, only the great feeling of helping someone in need. I could join the armed forces, but no, if I had to leave that might be considered an act of desertion. How about a policeman, a fireman or maybe even a doctor? No, they were needed, but only at certain times. Certainly not a lawyer. Then I accidentally stumbled onto a good idea.

I thought about Danny and how she had helped me get started in baseball that day. I liked playing baseball a lot. So, I went out to the ball field across from the brewery and sure enough, there were kids running bases and hitting pop flies, practicing for a game.

"Hi, Danny!" I greeted her, but she didn't seem to know me.

"Hi, yourself...who are you anyway?" she asked.

"I'm Phillip Ferguson, remember you taught me to play ball just a few weeks ago? I'm the one who hit that ball over into the glass window at the brewery."

"Really, I remember that guy, but you're not him...he was smaller... who are you really?"

"Could we sit down in the dugout, so I can explain something privately? Somehow when I first met you, I immediately thought you'd be my closest friend back then...but I got side-tracked, and here's the reason why."

Reluctantly, Danny followed me to the dugout and I told her everything.

"That's really hard to believe, Philly. That Philly was so young. Now you look my age, and I'm in high school. But, if what you say is true, you could prove it to me right now. Go catch this ball before it hits the ground," she hollered out trying to make a fool of me.

Danny stood up quickly and threw a baseball up high and as hard as she could, out into centerfield. Like a flash of lightning, I caught that ball up in the air and returned to her side, before she knew the ball hadn't touched the ground. We both were standing on home plate. I had her ball in my hand and she had her mouth wide open.

Other players who were looking out towards centerfield, were still discussing and asking one another what had just happened. We went back into that dugout. Danny was staring at me.

"We have to talk about this, Philly. You want to make millions of dollars? My dad knows some scouts and he can get you a tryout. You're a sure top prospect. Can I be your agent?" she rattled off excitedly.

"Well, yes, and no. I thought I could help save lives. I don't know how long I have left…remember? I told you, Dad's rats shriveled up and died. That might happen to me."

"Oh, no. How do you feel now?"

"Like a million bucks…what's that?"

"What's what?" she questioned.

"Can't you see those guys trying to steal that car?"

"Hey! That's my new car!"

"You're sixteen?"

"No, seventeen, two weeks ago…hey! Get away from my car," she hollered at the thieves, wielding her bat, while also dialing 911 and telling the emergency dispatcher to send the police to the park.

It was time for action, but I didn't exactly know what to do. Danny took off after the three car thieves. They weren't afraid of a girl, but stopped jimmying the door locks to address her approach. They all pulled out knives and advanced with their shiny steel blades.

I did the only thing I could think of and that was to take away all the knives right out of their hands and tie their shoe laces together. They suddenly all fell down helplessly and Danny held them at bay with her baseball bat above them, until the police came and took them away.

I stood beside her and helped intimidate them by retying their laces, so fast they got up and fell down so many times they just gave up. No one got hurt, but the policemen told Danny that these same guys had broken into other cars. She was getting a citation award for bravery from the police department. Now that's the way I liked it to go down. Nobody even suspected I had anything to do with it.

"Thanks…I saw what you did….you're amazing. Can I be your agent?" she asked again.

"First, if you become my agent…will you be there with me?"

"Gosh, I have my senior year in high school to finish. But if you say yes, I'll be at your games. If you play, it's only two or three hours on a game day, plus practices. You'll have lots of time to be Mr. Good Guy."

"That's what's most important to me. Okay, I'll ask Mom and Dad what they think. They're really smart people. Where can I meet you?"

"Looks like we always meet here. Tomorrow, I want you to meet my dad. He's really smart, also. He'll know what you can and can't do in baseball. Got cleats?"

"What?"

"Do you own a pair of baseball cleats…shoes?"

"Oh,…no, but I can buy some, I think."

"What size are your feet…those shoes look a bit small for you."

"Yeah, Mom bought them just this week and they were too big."

"Dad has lots of cleats. I'll have him bring some. You can buy them if you want, or your agent might do that if Dad thinks you're as great as I do."

Danny had a smile that made me feel good inside and, yes, I think I was getting a crush on her. But she was seventeen. And me, I was just one year old…go figure life out.

I discussed my happiness was being in baseball and Dad had some advice.

"Son, if you really don't want notoriety and lots of publicity, you had better take it slow and not go hitting those monstrous homeruns or everyone will bother you. I guess this means your mother and I get free ball tickets, huh? But I'm going to do more research for your condition. Go out and become the man your mother and I hoped you'd become."

I had good parents and they always gave learned advice. I decided to try out with Danny's dad.

I got a very good night's sleep and in the morning I walked on over to the ball diamond. I forgot Danny was in school, until it was lunchtime. Then I went back home and waited until five, then returned. There they were.

"Hey…Philly! Dad, this is Phillip Ferguson. He's why you're here. Philly, meet my pop," Danny gleefully presented us.

"Glad to meet you, son. How old are you? You look very young, but your physical appearance looks older."

"That's heredity for you. I graduated from that big college that has that golden dome."

"Notre Dame?"

"I have a degree in, well several things. I'm what they call a prodigy."

"Oh, you're about twenty-one then. Why haven't I seen you?"

"Oh, you have. You just didn't notice me on TV. I played football, not baseball. But, that's behind me. I want to play baseball now and I need your expert opinion as to my chances," I said.

"My daughter says you can knock the cover off the ball…can you catch?"

"I sure hope so, or I'm certainly wasting your time, huh?"

"I brought along some cleats from Rawlings. I sell these, and if you want them afterwards, I'll give you a good deal. Put on these, they look your size."

Mr. Strong was a really great person. Danny and I warmed up playing catch and I felt really good. I must admit that Danny burned that ball in my glove pretty hard and it stung sometimes.

Soon I was warm and Mr. Strong offered me his best outfielder's glove. I could buy that, too. Danny hit me several fly balls, then her dad hit some wowsers…they went far and up out of sight. Luckily, my speed got me to them and I caught every one. Mr. Strong was very pleased and right away he said I had an excellent arm, since I threw the ball all the way back in to Danny, so straight and so hard. She caught every one, too.

Then he had me run the bases. I had to be diligent and reduce my output, because Dad told me to not show anything highly unusual or I would be paparazzi bait. I asked Mr. Strong what was major league speed. When he said three seconds, I thought he meant three seconds all the way around the horn.

He was dizzy right after I lined up and he said, "Goooooo? I think I didn't see what you did. I had a dizzy spell. I clicked off three seconds. Honey, would you get me some water?" Mr. Strong asked Danny. He sat down on the bench. I went with Danny.

"How am I doing?"

"What do you think? You ran those bases faster than any human ever has. Dad just was timing your speed to first base. Run three seconds from home to first and you're a pro. Three seconds around the horn and you're superman," she said grinning.

I sure loved her smile and I hoped to see more of that.

After he regained his composure, Mr. Strong decided he would throw batting practice. After I hit all of their balls over the fence without effort, he said he was taking me to a tryout camp.

"Who do you want to play for?" he asked.

"If there's a choice for me…I best become a Saint Louis Cardinal, or my pop would murder me!" I said chuckling.

"Then we'll give them a call. How can I reach you…ah, what's your name again?" he asked, with his notebook out.

"I'm Phillip Ferguson…my friends call me Philly."

"Philly? Ha, a Philly trying out for the Cards. Amazing…how old are you?"

"I was born on October thirty-first, I'm almost three, in dog years," I laughed.

"That's twenty-one, Dad" Danny quipped.

Though it was a bit confusing, I tried my best to tell the truth. Mr. Strong gave me his card and told me to keep the shoes and glove. Danny gave me a hug and her cell phone number. I went home smiling. Danny left her smile with me.

The trip to St. Louis across the Poplar Street Bridge was exciting. We passed the Arch and I knew everything about it from my video sessions. It was the "gateway to the west", I remembered, but the next exit to the gateway off ninth street made me nervous. I actually walked through the Cards' players' entrance gate and then inside the office of the manager. He was a bit skeptical, but he was super smart not to look a gift horse in the mouth. I saw him shake hands and also heard him speak to Danny's father.

"Stone, you're the only reason I have faith in this guy. I know who brought me Albert. I'm waiting…get him a uniform and have him select a bat.

"Get warmed up, son," he told me. "Our practice pitcher is due in, in about an hour for early hitters. I'll try to work you in. You know… most guys go through the draft, then the minors. If you're as good as Mr. Stone tells me, well, let's just see first," he said, with a pat on my back.

As I dawned that uniform with no numbers on it, I saw one I

really liked. It was the bat boy's uniform. Bottle Baby…Bat Boy…a bit immature thinking, but I liked it. Now that would really be reclusive and I'd still be available. It fit just perfectly.

When the manager asked me to shag some fly balls out in center field, I found myself next to Jon Jay. He was a super star from the University of Miami and I had seen his speed and power on TV.

"How's it goin', bat boy?" he asked when I came to his side.

"Fine, sir…I'm here to try out."

I guess no player likes to think he's helping his competition, but he had lots to tell me.

"Look, get some shades on and look up into the sky before you make a fool of yourself. It's different inside here. Look, here comes one…I got it! Always call out a hit ball, if you can get to it, so you don't run into anyone…I got it!"

He caught another. He caught several more and I watched his style…he was good.

"Okay, I'm finished. Use my shades," he said handing them to me.

"Thank you, sir. I'll try my best."

"You do that, kid…go get 'em," he laughed.

Then the guy with the fungo bat cracked one really out of the park. I got a bead on it and caught it just before it cleared the left field wall. Immediately the manager came out of the dugout and said something to his assistant.

"Yo! Bat Boy…go get this one!" he hollered laughing out at me.

At the crack of the bat I saw he had tried to fool me and hit a ball so high, I don't think anyone could have caught it, except me. He had hit it straight up above home plate as he would have hit one for a catcher to catch. There was no catcher, so I zoomed up and caught that ball. Then I handed it to him smiling.

"Where in the heck did you get this guy, Stone…from a Russian pit full of radiated freaks? Hey, bub, try this one," he shouted to me as I was returning to the outfield.

That ball was hit really high and into left field. I did the old Willie Mays catch, catching a fly ball over my shoulder. Now suddenly I was having too much fun and all the players started watching me. I stood flat footed and threw a liner all that way, right into the catcher's mitt.

After shaking off the pain, he hollered out that it was terrific. I did it over and over for them.

It wasn't until I chased a fly ball over the centerfield wall and jumped up into a blacked-out area over the fence to catch it, that I realized I had done just what Dad had warned me. Photographers were coming down snapping pictures. I had ruined my plan in the first hour.

Then I was called in to play infield. I scooped up infield grounders at third, short, and including first base. I dazzled them with my play and then I was asked to hit. I had gone too far and couldn't help myself.

It was fun, lots of fun, but suddenly I felt sick. I hit everything they threw at me, including hitting a couple of those balls completely out of the new stadium. When that happened, the manager came running to me with Mr. Stone and they had papers to sign. I saw Danny smiling, but I was dying inside.

"Now don't get excited, but I think we might be able to use you in tonight's game. We'll have to talk to the guys upstairs…well, there they are now drooling over the rail looking at you. Anyway, we like the way you play and we'd like to sign you to our Memphis club. How's that sound?"

"I think it's wonderful and thank you for letting me try out, but…"

"But what! You want big money? Then we'll discuss it with your agent. Stone, are you signed with him?"

"No, but…"

"Danny Stone is my agent," I halfheartedly told him.

"What's wrong…something's wrong here…let's have it," the manager demanded.

"I just want to be your bat boy for now. I'm not ready yet."

"What! What's wrong? You're ready…have an aversion to flying first class, or staying in those big fancy hotels, all you can eat gourmet meals, nice cars, your own baseball card and kids wanting your autograph… wonderfully prepared meals and money to burn? What else is there?" he fumed.

"I just want to learn the game. I've only played in one game as a sub."

The strangest look came over the manager as he slowly turned to Mr. Stone.

"You got any more hidden talent with experience I should know about…say someone who's played, maybe two games?" he sarcastically questioned, a bit more confused than irritated.

"Boss, let me talk to Philly. I think he's right. Let's just ease off and when he's really ready, I guarantee you Danny will sign him, right, Danny?"

"I'll have to discuss this with my client. In the mean time, I'll see to it he gets more training and tell you his decision…it is his decision alone, not mine."

It was quiet all the way back home. Mr. Stone kept starting to say something, but Danny touched his arm not to, each time.

"Thank you, Mr. Stone. I hope I'm not upsetting you. I'll let you know very soon."

Then I smiled at Danny as they left. She motioned for me to call her. I saw a feud beginning between them inside their car before they left. I went in and washed up for supper and had lots to ponder. When I found out no one was home, I decided to just go take a hike…well, I just stepped outside and flew up into the sky.

I had a lot to consider. Was I really going to be a crime fighter, lifesaver-type, or a good example for kids and conquer what ever dreadfulness confronted me? I went higher than I had ever flown before, because I was thinking, until I looked down and a Boeing 797 jumbo jet flew right under me. Could that be? I dove back down to thicker air and just went zooming over St. Louis. Then I spotted the real Gateway to the West, so I landed.

As I sat atop of that shiny 630 feet tall St. Louis Arch, I looked out at the nighttime Cardinal's game going on below. The stadium was packed full, a sea of red, and the crowd was cheering for Albert. I was just daring him to hit one to me.

Albert apparently likes to please everyone, because I saw him step up to the plate and knock in his number four hundredth career homer. Now, really it was I who caught that ball. I put that ball in a special place, because I whizzed down, grabbed a ball out of the pitcher's bullpen, zipped back up, caught Albert's ball still in flight, while also dropping the bullpen ball over the fence. No one could even see me. I was pleased at my speed, and I'll cherish that ball for a while. Of course,

I'll give it back to Albert when he least expects it. I know one day he will be in the baseball hall of fame at Cooperstown.

Albert really is something. All the kids want to be like him, me, too. He was kind to everyone and he donates not only his time, but lots of his own money, very willingly, I might add. I guess he made up my mind for me. I wanted to be like him. But, there was only one Albert and I wasn't him. I wasn't going to replace him, even if I could.

I called Danny late and told her of my decision, but she was hesitant to agree, or say that she could get it done. She did ask me if I had a date for the junior-senior prom. I said I accepted, because I didn't attend her school.

Consequently, I agreed to sign that big contract someday, say in ten, fifteen years or so, with money to be determined later. Until then, I have become the bat boy for the Cards, just to disguise the original Bottle Baby on my uniform. I still like its character though, because Dad did this to me.

Every day in practice, every game day or night game, I rub elbows and get taught by the best. When you come out to Busch Stadium, take note of my quick return of foul balls to the umps and how quickly I can arrange all the bats for the guys. Nobody does it better. Best of all, I get to sit in the dugout.

These were my very first adventures in my first year of life. I love my parents and I love my country. When I feel ready, I'm going to step up to the plate and knock one out of the park just for you. I'll be aiming to hit one or two over the Arch, too. Until then, I hope everyone respects the bat boy. I'm having the thrill of my life...almost ready, too, when Albert calls it quits someday.

Oh, I almost forgot. Mom eventually discovered Dad's error in his procedure with his rats. It was two-fold. He gave them his mixture by bottle, but the additive by a shot in the keister. Therefore, the additive caused the rats to die, not the mixture. Since I hadn't received that shot, I was safe...that's my Mom!

THREE MONTHS WITH YETI BROWN

PREFACE

My landing was unexpectedly made too swiftly, for I bounced much too hard against a huge, jagged-edged granite boulder. I had come down Geronimo through the tall trees, falling right into the middle of an ice-cold, trout stream's creek bed. The fifteen hundred foot fall didn't hurt me, it was that sudden stop that did.

I screamed out in pain, as I was bounced and rolled, helplessly being dragged, squirming around, trying desperately to detach myself. I felt broken and dying, until I fainted and the lights went out. My face went below the icy water and that snapped me wide awake quickly. I was freezing to death under a warm sun.

The surrounding snowcapped mountains of the area were receiving the warmth of the late spring sunshine and had begun releasing ice water from their snow packed drifts from high above; rushing down thousands of feet into the valley streams where the rainbow, cutthroat, and brown trout swam; and now me, too. I eventually floated into deeper, calmer, smoother water.

Semi-conscious, numbing quickly and drifting with the flow, I let the swift current carry me to shallower water, until I got hung up near the shoreline. The icy overhanging fringes were sharp as glass, and without gloves, I just slipped off from my hold each time I tried to get up. Then I floated some more, until I hit a brush pile log jam.

I became hung up on a fallen dead tree limb. That limb kept me from floating further or dragging myself out onto the bank, both. I was helplessly pinned there, too weak to shake loose. The pain was torturous, and I feared by sundown I had seen my last sunset. The blood from the gash on my hip began to turn the water red around me.

Suddenly, I smelled a horrible stench. That ripe, skunk-ish odor made me fear the worst. Somewhere close by lurked a roaming grizzly. Apparently it had caught my blood's scent and I'd surely be eaten alive; right after he had violently ripped off my limbs, one by one, and wrestled with my body torso's carcass, like a toy.

I had seen and heard the "what to do" stories if a hungry bear attacks. Defenseless, no gun, no knife, and a severely broken hip, I knew there was only one thing left. I had to close my eyes and play dead, no matter if the bruin began to chew off one of my appendages. Bears like the struggling animal for a feast best.

First I felt a nudge on my head and heard the deep grunts. Then it was the tugging on my chute, which caused so much body pain that I almost screamed out. I continued playing dead, as I felt the grip on my arm. I was being dragged up out of that ice water. It dropped me onto a grassy ledge and my chute was thrown or landed over top of me.

I thought it was walking away, and when I peeked, I saw the immense body and the long brown hair. Then, that animal started covering my whole body with tree limbs and leaves, grasses and leafy bushes, until I was completely buried. It felt a bit warmer then, until it urinated upon me. I guess he left his scent behind to show other carnivores that I was his meal.

Helpless, I heard it shuffle away through the leaves. The animal left me then, but I knew its return would be at some more convenient time when he would come back to finish the job. Luckily, I passed out from the terrible urine stench, while desperately trying to hold my breath.

During that time of those long hours of torture while still helplessly buried beneath the debris, my entire life flashed before my eyes, in a wondrous, dream-like adventure.

CHAPTER ONE

From a hard working eighteen-year-old high school graduate, I evolved into a hard-studying, self-motivated, Midwest college student. Unfortunately, as some small town boys are, I was still very naïve for my age, but I was also very unaware that I was so inhibited.

The outdoor hunting magazines I read in my leisure time and most of the TV shows I watched, were attracting some of my personal attentions to their great adventures in the wild. Outdoor adventure magazines are full of exploration stories, some of which could make one's own hair curl, others explained the dos and don'ts of survival in the outdoors.

TV programs were often of a misadventure-type, where the narrator/writer suffered dire consequences, because of their limited lifesaving skills or outdated survival techniques. It was always explained further that he or she needed to have known how to survive in the wild outdoors in advance.

I lived daily on the premise that I eventually would become a hunting guide, but if nothing else, I wanted to become a true outdoorsman by any means. I dreamed of being an old-time adventurous explorer, just like a Lewis and Clark prototype.

Therefore, I studied most of the "how-to-survive this and how to survive that" by reading all the books I could lay my hands upon by the leading, famous, outdoor authors, but only after my own curriculum studies were met. I planned to be prepared so I continued to read all I could get my hands on in my spare moments.

I eventually became self-sufficient in snakebite treatment, venomous snake, bird, mammal and insect identification, broken bones and splinting, poisons, poisonous plants, edible plants and roots, starting fires and suffocating them, tracks left by animals both hoofed and wing and most importantly, reading maps and making a trail. I learned what to do after reading about getting lost. One should just try to follow a river or the sun. What I did not learn was how to die with dignity.

However, I would sometimes read with continuing discouragement that the last of our American pioneering frontier had long been gone for almost a century, except for the marine biology and oceanography science studies on the coastal Atlantic shelf and the deep offshore Pacific.

I presumed that my chances for that special adventure were diminishing rapidly or were already gone. Marine college curriculums bored me then, for I lived in the Midwest where no saltwater exploration obviously ever occurred.

Therefore, the direction my avenue of study took as I entered college was studying business administration as my major.

My general studies had included anthropology, biology, and English literature, among others; each subject seemed to maintain my internal fires burning and yearning, just enough to continue wanting to be an experienced explorer.

I concluded after my first two years in college were successfully behind me, that I would have to leave this wonderful continent and go to darkest Africa, or beyond, to fulfill my adventurous desires.

Additionally, each course I had taken played an integral part in my eventual learning. I planned to be prepared and continued to read all I could get my hands on in my spare moments.

On my ultimate trek into the deep woods, I would go out into the unknown, wherever I found it. I could not go searching for an animate or inanimate relic or object, no caves with hieroglyphics, or any secret passage to the forbidden jungle. Those had been found. I would just be searching for my own self-identity, entertainment, and self-satisfaction, knowing I tried to complete a dream of mine. I waited years for that opportunity to arise. It still hit me by surprise.

CHAPTER TWO

My first year of college began leisurely. I spent many uninterrupted hours inside my small dorm room playing Nintendo games against Oscar Polanski, my all-time Mortal Combat enemy. He was also my slovenly roommate from Chi-town, so nicknamed by me as Chewy, because he ate candy bars incessantly, and threw their wrappers down wherever he had not thrown one down before. Needless to explain, Chewy always left a visible trail to locate him.

I had accrued many games from family Christmases and birthdays, plus many more games of that era bought from the video stores. Nevertheless, those fabulous times were often disturbed, broken up sometimes by late-night cramming, sudden morning alarm clocks sounding, and fast treks across campus to my assigned classes for lectures and tests.

The college scene seemed so effortless, uncomplicated, and month after month becoming more mundane. I was not the social type. I did not smoke grass, do any drugs or stay out late searching our big campus for lonely girls.

On the other hand, I was not an introverted, self-sufficient nerd. Oh, I had plenty of women make advances, but I did not have the dough to meet their needs of flowers, expensive romantic dinners, and movies I knew they demanded.

Nevertheless, I was satisfied just the same, until my junior year. I was an A+ student, doing well in business administration. It was a field chosen by my college academic advisor, as a result, she told me, of my placement from my 1300 SAT's, 34 ACT score and mathematical expertise. I was unsure if I could have pursued a more amiable career and be successful. Nevertheless, business finance was certainly not garnering my interests. I still had daydreams of the wildwood.

In January, while seated in advanced American history class 305, an elective, Monica Wright became seated next to me. A computer selected our assigned seats alphabetically without choice. We were near the back of the auditorium, so placed there because of our last names' spelling. I was used to that placement for I had always been put to the rear of the class my entire school life. I guess it made me strain to understand better and that might have been beneficial.

On this particular day, my weary head was down, for I was still exhausted from my long, late night's drive back to campus, while returning from Christmas break. My month of freedom was about to end as I slid down into my seat and closed my eyes to listen.

I began to feel the vibes, which included, but were not limited to, the perfume fragrance from heaven, slight whimpers of rather sultry breathing spells with gasps, and continuous bumping and disturbance of someone's backpack carelessly being stuffed between my seat and theirs. Whoever arrived for theirs was noisy, so I moved over a bit to give up some space, but still kept my eyes shut.

I did not look up, but peeked open my eyes left, to catch a glimpse of the annoyance. What I discovered was a most beautiful co-ed, who looked like a Greek Row Goddess. She sat erect, staring at my nonchalant posture, which included the in-between armrest that she felt, was hers, not mine. When she bumped my arm and my head slid off my hand, I awoke from what I thought was another classroom daydream. I immediately sat up straight, just as the professor turned on his address system to begin.

"Hi," she said. "I'm Monica Marie Wright. I hope we can share this class by allowing the other to concentrate thoroughly on its content, without disturbing the other…you know what I mean?" she said rather arrogantly as she attempted to push my arm back off her desk.

"Yeah…I'm your worst nightmare, sweetheart, so just sit back and enjoy yourself. Make certain you have plenty of room while you're at it," I told her, offended because she was such a pushy snob.

I stood up in my seat and looked around for another, but the professor quickly reminded us all, as he looked directly at me, that the seating assignments were final, without exception. I smiled and sat back down.

For the next ten days of classes, I listened intently to the professor's lecture on our American heritage. It was quite interesting and when the next assigned five chapters included the Northwest Passage saga, I was even more enthralled. I did not take notes. After all, most of my classes were direct repeats of high school. I was a straight A+, 4.0 GPA student and also the valedictorian of my graduating class of four hundred twenty-five.

I just listened and watched, as my adjacent seated snobby witch struggled to take her notes, and break her pencil tips. It was amusing, but not as amusing as my A+ grade on the first test and her big fat F she got from the professor. She was very distraught, but more so when I allowed my A+ paper to fall onto her side of our desks.

"Sorry," I said, when her eyes grew wide after seeing my red A+ in disbelief.

I got up after class headed for my next, advanced calculus, when someone tugged on my parka's sleeve. It was the pushy snob.

"Hey…I guess I owe you an apology. Now that we respect each other, I hoped we could at least talk. I noticed you seem to understand everything in the class and I wondered if you had time for a soda or something so we could talk."

"Sorry, my next class starts in five minutes over at Nealy Hall. However, I consume lunch at twelve forty-five in the student center cafeteria. I can eat and talk then until about two."

"Oh, I have class then."

"Sorry then," I told her, as I turned to walk away.

"Wait! This is important. I have to have help with this history class or I will flunk it and lose my grant. Maybe you could see me after your evening meal. I thought you might be available to tutor me some, that's all. I'll pay."

"Sorry again! I have a big Nintendo challenge going on in my dorm room with my Mortal Combat enemy. I'm about to win the war!"

She looked downright disgruntled, as if she had never been denied before. Then she spoke in a more humble tone of voice.

"Please, let's start all over, okay? Friends call me Missy. I hale from Portland, Oregon. I am here on a federal student grant to research

Midwest soils and learn about some of the ecological systems used by the Chinese who farm here."

"Chinese?" I questioned.

"Yes, most people don't know it, but China has used our colleges and technology for years, but has also made great advancements in what they learned. China owns millions of Midwest acres and although our farmers grow their crops, their big industries, built right here on our soil, ship it all back overseas."

"You're kidding, right?"

"No, never…it's the absolute truth. I am here to learn and get my degree in forestry and minor in mycology. All of my mycology professors are Chinese-Americans.

"My parents are really tree farmers along the west coast. We grow birch for the drug companies. The warm rains build our forests quickly and assimilate Chinese weather…their same temperatures and rain totals. You see, we use their technologies, also, as they do ours. Our trees help them to develop new medical science. There's a secret inside those birch trees and it is why I need to learn about their knowledge of them.

"Our little plot is thirty-thousand acres of the most beautiful forests north of South America. However, we blend two groves; one is a faster growing, those are the fir trees, the other is the birch. We clear-cut fifteen hundred acres every year; process the birch trees into tiny chips, then into compressed bales to be shipped. The clear cut is then replanted that same year with trees to let stand for another twenty years, except for the fir and unless a forest fire takes it out. That's a lot of hard work. We ship mostly to the big drug companies here in the USA."

"What about the fir trees?"

"We ship them on semis all over in season. They're Christmas trees," she smiled.

"Wow…that's cool. I never knew that. So do you go out into those big woods and camp?"

"Sometimes, but it's hilly with deep valleys and rocky cliffs everywhere. The streams are cold and swift, full of native trout, which make great campfire dinners. It's a bit like what time forgot, if you know what I mean," she said somewhat apologetically.

This girl was after my heart and she did not even know it. It was my invitation, I hoped, to see the real deep woods, uninhabited by man. What a thrill it was just to think about it.

"Say, I agree. Why not come by my dorm apartment after six. My roomie is sort of a slob and has two evening classes tonight. I'll have time to clean up his mess and straighten up some."

"Hey…this isn't a date, remember…just study, okay?"

"Certainly…and you can tell me more about those deep valleys and cold streams. Is that where the hillbillies make moonshine? Oops, no, that's the Smokey Mountains, huh?"

"Yep. You drink, do ya?"

"No, just a passing thought I had. I must tell you, though, I have always dreamt about being a hermit in the deep woods of Alaska," I said chuckling.

"Fella, you help me get a good grade in history and you've got an invite to our place for a tour. It's not Alaska, but there's enough privacy to get lost and never be seen again. Dad says there are places in our hills where no man that he knows has ever been. How's that?"

"I accept. This is my lucky day," I told Missy.

She went east and I left west, late for my class and too late to get in. I decided it was fate. I could hurry home early, quickly clean up the apartment, and see to it that Chewy was gone to his classes on time. I did that almost every day anyway.

You see, Chewy was a rich kid from Evanston, near Chicago. He barely made it into the college scene and teetered upon academic suspension continually. His problem was not his intelligence; he was the laziest person I ever knew. Chewy always carried a big bankroll that was provided by his parents, which I tapped regularly in exchange for helping him write his papers and tutoring him through his business courses. Money for Chewy was no object, but a real problem for me.

Chewy's parents owned a big plastics factory in the Chicago suburbs and he hoped to be president of their company when his time came. Until then, he moped around college having a glorious time. I never met his parents, but I saw the big checks he demanded and received, whenever he wanted something.

Our dorm apartment, decked-out with the biggest large screen TV on campus and stacks of CDs, movies and girlie magazines, was the envy of every male student and all at his parents' expense. They liked me, because Chewy told them I helped him. Again, nothing was too pricey for Chewy.

To my dismay, Chewy was lying in his bed moaning from a big stomachache. I looked at the empty pickle jar on our kitchen table that we had four hamburgers. As of yesterday, it was full. I guess he ate them all on top of several Bit-O-Honey candies as several wrappers adorned our floor. How he never had acne or pimples, I have no clue as to why not.

"Brandon…thank goodness you're back. I have a gut ache and need help, now!"

I shook my head in disgust and went to our bathroom to get Alka-Seltzer. Plop, plop, and Chewy gulped the drink and passed bad gas. I opened the front door and put on the stove vent fan. That boy was ripe!

"Are you feeling well enough to go to class?" I asked.

"Oh, can't you see I'm still suffering?"

"Now that's a debate…you cut the cheese like a cannon and I can't get away."

"Surprise! Surprise! I was at Wal-Mart and bought some air freshener…here!"

Then Chewy began spraying an evergreen fragrance that was so strong I almost barfed. It turned out to be concentrated new car smell.

My college roommate, Chewy, was not what I expected when I signed a lease allowing the school to place him with me.

"Look, I have a nice girl coming over to tutor in history. If you're going to stay, please be quiet until she leaves, okay?"

"What about our big match on the tube?"

"That can wait. First, I have to pick up behind you. My gosh, did you eat ten candy bars?" I asked, still simply amazed while picking up and counting their wrappers.

"Yeah, if you go to the store, pick us up some health food bars. I think I'll go on a diet."

At 7p.m., Missy knocked on our door and I was surprised to see she had more than just the history book with her. She carried Algebra 101, Anthropology 101, American Lit 201, Geography 101, plus the 305 American History.

"Did you just finish those classes?" I asked.

"Well, actually, I brought these along just in case you might be willing to help me with those, also, if you will?" she asked smiling.

"Oh, sure I can. Sit yourself down at the kitchen table. I've already had those classes. I'm a junior, remember? My general studies are finished and now comes the important decision as to discover how I can totally screw up my life by taking more mundane courses, which I'll never need, in a career degree I'll probably hate doing forever, ha!"

"You hate your chosen career?" she questioned.

"I guess...I'm not sure, but, if you don't mind, I also tutor my roomie in two of those same books, so would you mind if he sat in for a while?" I suggested.

"Certainly...why not?" Missy agreed.

As soon as I summoned Chewy, there were sparks. Not love sparks, but the kind that causes havoc, even though he came with handfuls of pure chocolate candy Easter eggs that he loved so dearly.

"Oh, it's you! If he's your roommate, not only do I pity you, but I'm out of here!" Missy said, rising from the kitchen table chair, frowning at Chewy as he entered.

"Hey, babe! Want an egg? You hangin' out in the slums nowadays?" Chewy greeted her rather sarcastically.

"Look you, I don't have to put up with this, or you!" Missy shot back.

"Wait a minute here, wait just a minute! What's going on?" I begged, trying to get in between them before fisticuffs began.

"This guy is uncouth! He sits in front of me in anthropology and lets gas fly all class long. I hit him with my books and I was expelled from class, while he remained. Luckily, I switched classes and hours. You, you, uncouth animal!" she screamed.

I took Chewy back into his bedroom and asked him to shut up and stay there. This meant a lot to me, more than being his roommate, so he flipped on the TV, opened a giant Hershey bar and settled back to watch the Simpson's.

Missy was ready to leave as I returned, but I asked her to stay if she really needed help. Reluctantly, she sat back down.

"I know what you mean about Chewy," I whispered very lowly. "He has this medical problem and I don't know how long he has left," I continued with a little white lie.

"You mean, you mean…he can't physically help his condition… what is it?" Missy sorrowfully whispered.

"Carmelsplenditis, I think they call it. It's a rare affliction."

Of course, I made it up.

"Oh, I'm sorry. I guess I should apologize, huh?"

"Nah, I'll explain everything to him. He's really a nice guy with his brain misplaced."

"You mean his brain causes his problem?" she continued to mourn.

"Something like that…let's get to your homework," I suggested.

Missy was nice and she listened and learned well. Then I saw her squinting when she tried to read a passage out of the classic "Tales of Two Cities". I then asked her to explain, but she still squinted, as she looked at the book.

"Missy…do you wear glasses?" I inquired of her eyesight.

"No, never!" was her retort.

"Oh, don't get angry, please. I see you are squinting a bit. Here, try my reading glasses…go ahead…no one will see you…just a test," I encouraged her, until she slipped them on.

By her expressions, Missy seemed to act as if a completely new world had opened up to her. I suggested she take advantage of the school's free vision testing.

"Hey…I did," I mentioned. "Besides, you look very nice wearing glasses, intelligent, too…even in mine. Imagine you having Sarah Palin style rims…you'd look a lot like her," I hinted.

"Who's Sarah Palin?" she asked.

"She was only the hottest governor in the USA…Alaska! That's my favorite state. She was every young guy's dream girl way back when… unfortunately though, she had a handsome husband and about a half-dozen kids. Here she is in the newspaper. It's not a great pic, but you'd look like that, kind of, and I bet you'd see much better," I explained nicely.

"I must admit, I can see a lot better. Think I look freaky?"

"Nope…not at all…you look hot! That does it…Saturday we will both see Dr. Franklin at the student center. I need my eyes checked, too. Reading a lot tires the eyes and even a good night's sleep doesn't help if you have to read a long novel," I tried to explain.

"Looks like I'm getting the best deal out of this. I get a friend, a tutor, and someone to take care of me. Gosh, I sure misjudged you, didn't I?"

"Well, I thought you were just a witchy snob, so I guess we both found out something nice here, huh? First impressions are sometimes deceiving."

We settled down to studying for two hours and after Missy was happy that she had come, learned what she needed to know, it was time for rest and relaxation.

"Come on out, Chewy!" I yelled.

"Let's get ready to rummmmmbllle!" he yelled, as he returned from the bedroom.

On popped the big screen and in went the video game. The battle was on. Mad button attacks led to sore thumbs and tiring hands. After many hard fought skirmishes and retreats, bugle-blowing charges, land mine explosions, bazooka blasts, tank overruns and troop decimations, the white flag rose over Chewy's brigade. I was triumphant. Through victory go the spoils. In my exuberance, I turned to Missy and surprisingly got a short hug.

To my astonishment though, she then patted Chewy on the shoulder to comfort his dismay and hugged the defeated Chewy longer. I sat back to watch them then knowing we had a mutual friend in Missy. She somehow had forgiven my uncouth roommate. Missy now was suddenly willing to overlook his slovenly ways, as I always had. She even ate some of the chocolate he offered. Chewy had apparently melted her heart.

Then as we all sat together on the couch drinking Cokes, I begged Missy to tell me more about the deep green forests of Oregon. She fulfilled my every dream about being out in the wild, as she told Chewy and me of the deep hidden caverns that were lush with tangled undergrowth, great for hiding bear, elk, bobcat and sometimes wolves and mountain lions.

There were fast running brooks, some filled with trout, some salmon, in cold icy streams, which one could literally bend down and drink up from its pure waters.

There were sudden eruptions in the Earth, where huge metamorphic rock jutted straight up into the sky thousands of feet from pressures exerted by the Earth's crust mantle shifting. Sometimes these rocks were made of sandstone and easily deformed by wind and water erosion.

Nevertheless, it was there that the guts of the Earth were exposed. There were hundreds of millions of years of deposits; it all intrigued me.

That territory hadn't been tapped for forestry agriculture, because of its inaccessibility. Thousands of acres were up higher into the mountains she proclaimed, all of which were actually untouched by modern man. Her father had inherited the area from an old land grant deferred to him by ancestors dating back to the Astorians of the early 1800s when the British explorers proclaimed it uninhabitable and bequeathed it to whoever was desirous of wanting the mass of rocks and trees.

"As told to my father," Missy explained, "the British explorers of the Columbia River thought our property a lost venture though it bore much wild game like otters, minks, elk and deer. However, those animals trapped more easily closer to the Pacific, and trappers readily traded their huge catches to fur companies along the coast. The fur companies shipped their products in abundance to China and the Far East. There was no need to rough it into that back country territory and fight the Indians and wild beasts.

"It has been in our family ever since," Missy continued. "My family has withheld all government and mining trespassers away. Because traveling there is extremely hazardous. Nobody really wanted it until the fungi findings by the Chinese."

Missy went on to tell us many things about Oregon's forestry and backwoods. Some of her parent's logging operations entailed the use of rigged pulleys and long cables that stretched a half-mile from mountaintop to mountaintop, where harvested trees actually flew through the air into camps.

At the camps, men examined them, sawed them up, and then forced them into their big mechanical chippers, which then chewed them up into tiny bits. After the chips were sacked up in thick plastic bales, they were hauled out on semis to wherever.

However, once they discovered a blackened residue of fungi inside the birch in abundance. At first they thought it was like a Dutch Elm disease and all the affected trees were burned.

However, visiting Chinese investors saw this fungus and knew the fungi's worth to them. Each tree had to be inspected to determine its worth. Hidden beneath the white bark is a medicinal-type fungus known to grow only upon the interior of the bark of the white birch, which drew drug company buyers' orders. After workers stripped off that residue into separate containers, the rest was used for its lesser chemical value for such things as bug spray repellant.

It was eleven o'clock when I suddenly noticed the time. As Missy gathered her books, I offered to walk her home, but Chewy had already thought of that and they both left without me.

I guess things had really changed in Chewy's life rather suddenly. For several weeks following, I came from classes to find Chewy had gone to his own classes on time. Our apartment had no candy wrappers thrown about either.

Apparently, the love bug had hit Chewy and he was a new man. He began to shower regularly, dress nicely, and his mid-semester academic reports were much improved to all above C+ grades. It was phenomenal!

Chewy also began spending much of his time studying. Missy came very regularly to be tutored and Chewy was right there actually listening intently. In addition, when Chewy's academic suspension warning notice was canceled, we all celebrated at the student union building by bowling.

It was during my run to the sandwich bar for refreshments that I noticed a colorful poster tacked onto the student employment bulletin board. It read that large groups of history students, along with several professors were tracing the trail of Lewis and Clark's expedition and there were vacancies for additional student participants. I was immediately concerned, until I saw the expense. I did not have that kind of extra money.

The cost was $6,500 for the three-month summer's trek up the Missouri River, with farther foot exploration along the trail into the area of the Northwest Passage. Additionally, college credit was being attached to the event; nine hours of credit for three 400 level advanced history courses, as well as self-preservation techniques were being taught.

All outdoor supplies were furnished such as tents, backpacking gear and even toilet paper. Gosh, where would one be without at least that modern convenience, I mused to Missy and Chewy who came to see what held my attention from returning with our refreshments.

"You want to do it, don't you, Brandon?" Chewy suddenly spoke looking directly at me after he, too, read the poster.

I smiled, but he could see through my look of disappointment. He knew I could not afford such an event.

"Hummm, I think I'd like to do it, too. However, if my best friends don't go, I won't. I have a sneaking suspicion Mom and Dad will be thrilled because of the grades the registrar's office sent them. I bet that next semester's check will be more than enough to cover that trek for us all. They last told me I could buy a Corvette, if I got off academic probation. Heck, I'm in 'good student' status now…they'll cheer hallelujah! I'll call them now to see if they got the great news… wait here a minute," he said, as he sought a quieter corner.

Chewy was all smiles as Missy and I watched him talk to his parents on his cell phone. He hopped around like a nut in the bowling alley, causing people to stare at him compellingly, as they tried to concentrate on their bowling. Then he returned with the biggest smile on his face.

"Hey, believe it or not, I'm now rich! Dad put a quarter-million in my account, partly because it's some of my twenty-first birthday's inheritance last month and partly because of my new interest in making something of myself.

"Business is booming in Chicago. Mom and Dad both liked the expedition idea as long as I got college credits. They told me to live off that for a year and there would be more forthcoming. He and Mom actually told me they were proud of me and loved me. Now that's a first! They told me, Brandon, to tell you thanks, also. So, my friends, let's go sign up!"

"I'm very sorry for you," Missy softly spoke. "If that was the first time your parents told you they loved you, you must have been a very lonely child," she explained.

"Hey, you have it all wrong. My parents show their love by providing me with what I need and more since they are rich. I know they love me…I think," Chewy quipped, then his demeanor suddenly changed. "You think they just want to keep me away?" he then asked looking at us both.

"Nonsense! You are just now acting like a normal person and they're shocked, that's all. I read their letters and they always sign off, 'Love, Mom, and Dad', right?"

"Yes!"

"Well, then…they love their little boy, I think."

"Yeah, I guess they do. Now let's go sign up on that trip!"

"Oh, I really can't," Missy quickly told Chewy.

"Why not?" he asked.

"First, it wouldn't be right, and secondly, I have a summer job at my parents' business. They are depending on my new knowledge here to teach Dad and the others what I learned about how to improve our soils and trees. They, too, are glad of my good grades. Nevertheless, you two guys should go. If you get up as far as the Pioneer Pass, then you're at my backdoor. Call me from there. That's as far as anyone is legally allowed to proceed. I never knew of anyone who ever got even that far, but you two might. I'll be looking forward to hearing from you along the way. But I can't go this time, not yet," she informed us.

"We'll have to think hard on this one. Let's first bowl our last two frames," Chewy told Missy and me.

After bowling, Chewy walked Missy back to her Greek Row Sorority and returned telling me she was the girl he would marry. I was happy for the guy, but I wasn't sure Missy felt as he did about their relationship. Still I wished him well, as he headed off to shower.

Later, Chewy poked his head out and just said goodnight. Enchanted, caught up in the thoughts of how I could ever afford that school-sanctioned trip, I then fell asleep dreaming of the wonderful wilderness that I might see.

Missy's words kept crossing my brain. I thought of those streams of fish, and trees so tall you could not see their tops. The rock that jutted straight up in some places, she said, made it impossible to go any farther. I wanted to be there; the place time forgot and modern man had not left his footprints.

CHAPTER THREE

It was soon spring quarter's end, also the last days of May. All of our finals were over. Each of us excelled academically. During all that time however, my mind was overrun by thoughts of being free. Free to roam the deepest woods in the heart of Oregon.

Our friend Missy had finished sooner than Chewy and me. She already had left to drive back to her Oregon home, before Chewy got up enough nerve to buy her a ring. All of his dates had been threesomes with Missy and me, so I wondered just how he had arrived at the idea she was the one for him.

After Chewy could not persuade me to accept his gift offering for my $6,500 fee to attend the tag-along trek up the Missouri River, and through Kansas, Nebraska, Wyoming and into Oregon country after three months, he decided not to go either. However, when I showed him that this trip was meaningful to his educational transcript and would put him past his three previously failed classes, he reconsidered everything.

"Look, Chewy, if I come up with the monetary necessity, I'll hop on a plane and fly out to Cheyenne or close by and join you. But if I don't, tell Missy hi for me on those long, lonely walks into her parents' woods."

That was all the encouragement needed to convince Chewy. He then concurred and began packing for his trip. The next afternoon, I went with Chewy to see him off on his exploration caravan.

I spoke with Professor Martin, one of my past instructors, and wished him well. I told him how I envied him, but I didn't have the funds. He said if I had a change in my status just call Chewy and we could meet up someplace. I hadn't even considered that happening.

"You were my top student. I hoped you'd have come along. We'll be leaving for St. Louis, Missouri by bus. There, several other college professors and I, plus about thirty pioneering Southern University students are being taken out to get onto an assemblage of docked houseboats. We all are to use those while moving up the Mississippi north of St. Louis, then off west from the Mississippi and up the Missouri River. That's where the real expedition begins at the end of river travel. We'll be hiking from there using our GPS coordinates. Well, got to get going...wish us luck," the professor asked.

"Good luck, Chewy...you all take care of him for me!" I said, as the bus pulled away.

My intentions then were to call my loving parents and tell them I was doing a student summer-work-program, collect some cash, and head home until fall classes began. I could usually get a campus job as a painter and the football stadium now needed repainting.

However, I met John DuPree, another soon to be senior. He was a pilot and belonged to the Midwest Hi-Jumpers, a group who met monthly at the hometown airport to practice parachuting. John asked me if I was interested in working at the airport weekdays as a behind-the-counter, ticket-taker, small order cook, and bottle washer of sorts. I would also serve sodas and cook hamburgers. It was an hourly stipend, which included a cot to sleep on overnight in the backroom. He said I could make about three thousand over the summer, which included all the hamburgers I could eat. I decided to take the job, because my interest in airplanes was almost as great as the call of the wild.

It was Sunday, as I exited my church, John Dupree came up beside me.

"Hey...didn't see you here before."

"It's my third year, I beg your pardon."

"Well now, we do have a common bond as we both believe, huh?"

"Yep, I know I do."

"Feel like going up today?"

"What do you mean, 'going up'?"

"I'm flying today. Some of the guys and girls jump every weekend. I volunteer my jumper plane...a twin-engine de Havilland DHC-6."

"Sounds serious…sure, I'd like to do that."

"Just follow me back to the airport and I'll fit you for a rig. You might want a free ride with Big George."

"Who's Big George?" I needed to know.

"That's what we call the harness to attach you to another trained and seasoned jumper. It straps you to them and you both go out at the same time. It's fun, if you really want to learn how to jump."

"Actually, John, I meant learn to fly. I don't know if I'm brave enough for jumping."

"After you're up for a bit you'll get your confidence. If not, I'll help push you out, ha!" John said laughing, but I felt he really meant it as we drove out to the airfield.

The Sunday airport traffic was filling the parking lots and taxi areas with customers and visitors who evidently came just to enjoy the weekend activity on the runways. Often, cross-country flyers literally dropped in to refuel or have a lunch. It was then I got help as several college co-eds came in to bus and cook. I was the weekday person all by myself. Today I could rest. Then my cell phone summoned me.

"Hello!"

"Brandon…this is Chewy…how's it hangin', roomie?"

"Just got out of church, headed to the airport at Huey Field… what's up?"

"Are you going to fly out already?"

"No, I took a job out here for the summer…how are you?"

"We're floating on the Missouri for the next few days. We're having a ball. There are twice as many guys as girls, but you should see the scenery."

"Nice, huh?" I questioned, assuming he meant the river and wildlife.

"Yeah, three adorable juniors, all about my age and they play a guitar and sing Kumbaya around the campfire. We docked last night on a sandbar. It was super. We had a luau and I learned to limbo. The professors have not said anything about homework at all. I think it's called a self-learning adventure. So far, I've learned a lot though…I learned I needed lots more mosquito repellant and never to pee off the bow into the wind."

I almost split a gut, because that is just the antic I suspected to come from Chewy. He suddenly had to go and said he would keep in touch. I began to feel the desire to be out on that river with him, but that soon subsided when a nice single engine Mooney dropped down onto the runway just as I parked beside John at a hangar.

"Nice bird, huh?" John said, as we watched the Mooney touch down then taxi our way.

The engine whined, and then the prop shut down. A gorgeous woman stepped out from the cockpit door and hopped off the wing. When she removed her helmet and shook loose her hair, I swear she resembled an angel from heaven in a jumpsuit. Then she started walking our way with the widest smile of perfectly white teeth, I had ever seen.

"Morning, John!" she greeted.

"Morning, Jenny. This is Brandon Webb. He's our new weekday master flight attendant. Jenny, you gonna jump today?"

"That's why I'm here. Things at Dallas got boring, so I took off this morning and decided to stay for a while. You still got that good mechanic on call...Carl what's his name?"

"You mean Carl Neff?"

"Yes, I need an annual on my bird and I thought I could slip in and out in a few days here. Fort Worth was stacked up. Did Sally come in yet? We talked and she's coming down close to noon. When you plan on starting?"

"After I get Brandon here taught on the nomenclature of a silk...he might even jump Big George today. You wanna be his first?"

She looked at me closely, and then asked if I got sky sick, but I couldn't answer fast enough.

"I don't want to go through that again," she said still apparently judging my capability.

"What Jenny means, Brandon, is that not too long ago we had a real scare. Jenny is one of our top parachutists and she took a college girl up. Halfway down, the girl freaked out, puked right in her face and eyes and she entered deadfall. That means Jenny couldn't see a lick before they hit. But, our girl here did what I taught her, she smelled her way down."

"How can you smell your way down?" I asked.

"She didn't want to take her last breath, so she breathed deeply through her mouth for air changes. The air gets thicker and warmer the closer you get to the floor. You'll see. She glided in like a bird. She was messy, but she came down like an angel," John said putting his arm around Jenny.

"Let's grab a bite and then get Brandon some silk," John told Jenny.

We all strolled over to the canteen, but I never got a word in edgewise. It was a nice crowd inside and I decided to leave John and Jenny to their jumping and airplane jargon to say hey to the girls who were taking my place for the weekend. They buzzed around and finally one girl asked me what I wanted.

"Hi, I'm Brandon Webb. I'm the weekday help here. I thought I might bone up on what and what not to do."

"What you should have done was peeled and sliced up the onions ahead of time and put them in the fridge for us to serve, but I already took care of that. I just smell like an onion when I serve. I explained to the customer that our day cook forgot to do it. Hi, I'm Shelly," she then smiled and left too quickly with a tray of food.

"Well, actually… I haven't had a chance…" I spoke softly to no one.

No one stopped to listen, so I returned to John and Jenny. Then John received a call and said he would be back in twenty minutes, or so.

I stayed with Jenny, but she wanted to go back out onto the tarmac to secure her Mooney. I got my first look inside a really cool bird. Jenny let me slide in beside her, as she gave me a brief, but thorough account of every instrument, and there were at least fifty.

Then we went over to the hangars and saw John's big bird. It was huge and had little parachute decals by the dozens on the aft. Those were John's little flying achievements, Jenny related.

"John must like you," Jenny began, as we sat on lawn chairs outside in the shade under the hangar's overhang. "I guess we can hookup today after we fit you. I think you'll do fine," she continued as though it was my idea to learn to jump.

"How do we come down?" I asked.

"Safely," she laughed. "I'll have my arms around you tightly…we'll be locked up."

I looked at her and imagined what a wonderful thought that could be…Jenny and me, floating together up yonder in the blue.

"How high will we be?"

"About 3,500 for a three minute thrill," she quipped. "Think you can get it off by then?"

"What do you mean, get it off?" I was hesitant to ask.

"Silly, your blown mind…you'll get the thrill of your life and after the first time, we won't be able to hold you down," Jenny assured me.

John returned to the hangar with five other flyers and jumpers. A girl named Sally exited a bright blue and yellow Stearman stunt plane after she had just completed a perfect 360 degree barrel roll down the runway, which brought cheers and applause from the gathered crowd.

The spectators had now gathered about the lawn in camp chairs, watching the planes come and go. Then, everything seemed to stop, in the air that is.

Several people with aero planes, little tricycles with parachutes attached to a motor bearing a prop, took off three at a time and flew for a few minutes. A few more cranked up and began using the entire field as their runway. The airport was now closed to other traffic, while the skydivers got a chance to prepare. An unexpected experimental ultra light flew in off onto the grass and the pilot apologized for being late.

Meanwhile, back at the hangar, John and Jenny began teaching me the ins and outs and parts of a chute. I weighed in at 180 lbs., so I received an appropriate chute and jumpsuit that fit snuggly. I was also fitted with one of John's old helmets, but was told I would have to purchase my own for the next time…if there was a next time, I prayed.

A buzzer went off as the hangar doors slowly slid open. John, Jenny and I, along with six other suited-up parachutists sat inside John's big blue de Havilland. I was seated beside John, as his copilot when we taxied out onto the tarmac.

Surprisingly, the huge engine purred smoothly, just like a small tractor's engine. After his preliminary checks, there was clearance from the small tower that he was clear for takeoff. I felt the surge of the engine's power and almost immediately we were traveling seventy-five mph down the runway and rose very gracefully up into the sky.

After John banked his plane off left over the big adjacent farm field, the plane began a slow climb in a big wide circle. I looked at the altimeter as we leveled off at 8,560 feet and circled the airfield. The people's faces below could be clearly seen looking up at us. It was thrilling. Though I had been up before in big jets, nothing compared to hovering so closely to Earth. My love for this began.

"Your plane," John suddenly spoke and got up from his pilot's seat to address the occupants behind us and ready to jump.

My heart stopped, I think. I grabbed the wheel and hung on tightly in a sudden daze. Then John turned around to see my excruciating look of fright and said, "Relax…it's on auto-pilot."

I still held on but looked down to see if we were still up there. After a brief review of safety precautions to the jumpers, John sat back in his pilot's seat and took over. He yelled out, "Ready in five, four, three, two, one, good luck!"

On good luck, all but Jenny exited. One after the other jumped. I looked down upon them as each colorful silk chute exploded open into fullness and everyone was quickly whirling in big circles above the grass next to the airfield. As we watched the last chute land safely, and gather his silk, John took his plane down to 3,500.

"Ready?" was all he asked. "Go to the back, now," were his orders.

Before I could say, "Please, let's just talk about this some more," Jenny took my hand and snapped me into Big George next to her. She gently bumped me towards the opened door and then I felt her arms around me.

In an instant, before my mind could tell me I was scared as heck, out we both went. The sudden jerk of the chute opening caused me to look up to see if the chute had really opened and if the lines were going to snap from the jolt.

"Relax, Brandon, I've got you. Just let me take you to that place I told you we were headed and enjoy the ride. We're safe," Jenny assured my mind.

It seemed like she took extra care to allow me to look around, feel the freedom of the fall and the wind in my face. I didn't feel sick at all. When Jenny's legs pushed mine up over hers, we suddenly stopped four feet above the grass and we just put our feet down on terra firma, as the chute collapsed beside us. It was the most exhilarating experience I had ever known. And yes, I wanted to do it again, right then.

John flew in gracefully as more jumpers came to his running plane this time. I counted twelve. Jenny had left unhooking from me and repacked her own chute in minutes to join the throng. I waddled over to a camp chair in the Big George harness and sat watching John take the next group up into the air. His plane seemed much higher overhead when I heard its engine's noise go silent.

Suddenly, every jumper deployed in a stream of bodies. The sky filled with little streaking dots hurling at great speeds toward Earth. It seemed none of the chutes had opened and I stood up concerned. Several seconds passed and I became a bit alarmed. There was some sort of gathering up there. Suddenly they all dispersed at once, in every direction.

Then, one by one, every chute found a place to safely open and the show began. There were chutes with colored smoke spewing from the heels of their operators. Several had American flags fluttering behind them. One person actually did a summersault in the air as several seemed to hold hands and swirl in a circle together like they were square dancing for just a moment.

Soon, they all hung above us as if they were not coming down. Nevertheless, as they glided about, I could see the big smile on Jenny's face from below. I was not only very impressed; I was hooked.

With my jumping finished for the day, I watched three more leaps of faith, as I called it. Finally, John's de Havilland moaned as it came in like a big goose and settled softly on the tarmac. The hangar's big sliding doors opened and I had to get out of the way, as he taxied his plane back into its space in the hangar.

Then all the jumpers crowded around a social potluck dinner inside and listened to Jenny and John congratulate one of the jumpers who set some sort of record. Everyone was close and each discussed their thrills they had that day and the sales of newer chutes and more classes. The camaraderie was very strong. I liked that.

I sat back and enjoyed a sloppy Joe with chips and baked beans. Then Jenny came over and sat next to me.

"Hey…thanks for the great ride. I guess you were right. I can't wait for the next opportunity," I told her.

"Do you have your license lined up, yet?" Jenny asked.

"I need a license?" I questioned.

"Yeah, sure, and lots of training and more practice jumps with a partner. That's just the beginning. Say, I'm here for three days. I'd like to help you get your start. I have my old beginner's book and outlines still packed inside the Mooney…where you staying?" she asked.

"Here, I sleep in the canteen's backroom."

Jenny looked concerned. "Oh, I thought I might use that bed while the mechanic gave my ride its annual."

Jenny then stared at me and smiled.

"Well then, okay. I'll sleep in my car. I've done that lots of times. However, you'll have to wake me at five when I open up the place. I've only just gotten here and I don't have an alarm clock. My roommate took it with him. I only first start tomorrow morning. I'm not sure I can cook well enough either," I admitted embarrassingly.

"I guess I'll find out, huh? Tell you what. You give me your cot and I'll tutor you for your tests, while you get started and give you some cooking pointers. The rest is up to you. Wait here, I'll go get my pack and those beginner's notes."

John somewhat disappeared as Jenny settled down with me to go over her books and notes when she returned. She began immediately by showing me first-hand about the parts of her parachute, which I needed to know as she repacked her own. I found out about the D-bag, the center cell, the end cells and the front leading edge and trailing edge. It all seemed so simple, as Jenny asked me to explain each part. I found the stabilizer, the slider, front, and rear risers. I showed her the steering lines, steering toggle brake, and finally the body straps.

"What's this?" Jenny pointed out.

"Ah, that's the bridle line which attaches to the pilot chute, I believe."

"Amazing. You just went through a week of classes in an hour. That is really good, Brandon. How'd you do in school, anyway?"

"Valedictorian," I humbly told her.

"That figures! Let's get some drinks and you can help me get into your bunkhouse. We can sit in the canteen and continue. Heck, I'm thrilled you're so smart. Maybe you can get that license faster than I thought. But, we won't sacrifice practical safety, now will we?"

"By the way, how much will this entire license stuff cost? I'm working here at the canteen just to earn extra money for my last year at Southern. I had other plans though."

She hesitated to tell me then said, "It usually costs students $3,500 minimum for six weeks ground and their first five jumps; again that much in the air to be H certified. Moreover, you will probably want to be a pilot by that time. You'll have a leg up being a diver."

"Well, that ruins it. I can't get that kind of dough, until I graduate next year and find a job as a teacher or accountant somewhere."

"That's too bad, Brandon. I feel you'd get a lot of enjoyment from this. We can still work together on this while I'm here. I like your company. Maybe something will come up and you can still get your yellow card."

"You know what?" I told Jenny. "I've always had this deep yearning to go out into the wilderness and live like a hermit. Right now, I'm working toward that thought. It is something I just have to do. I missed a great chance just a few days ago to be on a college trek along the Oregon Trail route. I have a friend who promised me she would show me her dad's tree forests. The way she spoke, its way outback from civilization and just my speed. Can you understand that?"

"Actually, no…but I had a dream once of being a commercial pilot when I was just a little girl. I once looked up into the sky and saw a big plane overhead making white streaks in the sky. Of course that's the heat from the engines, but then I thought it was a special signal for me to follow my dream."

Jenny and I hit it off pretty well. We talked, laughed, and became very close. However, John never returned that night. The weekend help left me written orders for food for our next weekend's menu and surprisingly everything was left in its place and clean.

At eleven, I met Don Meyers who was on duty in the tower until the airfield closed. I never even knew he was there. He was a high school principal in a nearby school district and enjoyed his responsibility.

"See you all next week," Don called going out the canteen door.

Then, Jenny and I were alone. She poured us each a cup of coffee and we talked more and discussed all she could tell me about chutes until one in the morning. Then she went off to sleep in my cot. When I followed her, she was concerned, until I dug out my old sleeping bag. I dropped it behind the salad bar on the soft carpet and eased up under the food tray slide. However, I got back up when the lights glared too much that had to be kept lit.

I hung an extra sheet on the slide to block out the night-lights, and made a nice little tent. It wasn't bad until the ice maker churned out new ice at three o'clock and scared me half to death. Nobody saw me jump up and hit my head hard on the stainless steel tray slide above. That calmed my nerves and I immediately laid back down trying not to cuss. Morning came too quickly. I wasn't going to sleep there again.

CHAPTER FOUR

I got up at five; Jenny hadn't awakened me as I planned. I started up the coffee pot and turned on the stove to heat up the grill. I wanted to be prepared to serve breakfast to anyone who came in.

However, I had to wait until seven for my first customer, when Mr. Neff the mechanic came in for coffee, orange juice, two eggs over easy, two burnt toast and bacon. He ate his breakfast here each morning before going off to the hangar, he explained, and he asked for the newspaper. It was still outside, so I dashed out to get that.

The customers' tables were set up in the canteen with utensils wrapped in paper napkins, but Mr. Neff told me he always ate at the counter. I dawned my cook's hat and eventually asked him if he would settle for scrambled eggs, since I had allowed the grill to get a little too hot. I promised to improve. He was congenial and took my offering pretty well. At least I got the burnt toast just right. However, the coffee, well, I could not ruin that.

Jenny came out from behind the kitchen and sat down with Mr. Neff to discuss her annual FAA check-over on her Mooney. I heard him tell her he was busy for ten days, but he would place her bird next in line. He was the FAA inspector, also.

"Good morning, Brandon," Jenny greeted me when I finally came out from behind the grill. "Looks like we'll have lots of time to study that sky diving exam," she advised me. "Thanks for giving up your bed. Tonight I am going to a hotel. There are just too many noises around this place at nighttime," she let me know smiling.

I guess she did hear me hit my head.

Then Mr. Neff told me that he regularly ordered that same meal for his breakfast and gave me a tip. However not what I anticipated.

"Practice, practice, practice!" Mr. Neff said in leaving.

A Cessna flew in at nine with two executives who wanted petrol, so I found out I was the gas pump guy, also. John forgot to mention that, but Jenny knew where the gas pump keys were to the lock. She showed me what to do and how not to spill gas on the plane's fuselage by draining the hose before I took it out. That was simple enough.

Those were my only customers for the entire day. My first full day was a breeze.

Day after day, I became more efficient around the canteen. On my down time, Jenny grilled me on her own ideas of what I should know, all while her Mooney was being fitted with a newer Navcom radio system and several newer instruments.

"You know what a What-fo is, Brandon?" Jenny asked.

"A What-fo? Nope, never heard of such a thing."

"A What-fo is a guy who stands at the airplane's door, ready to jump, then changes his mind. He says, 'What-fo I want to jump out of a perfectly good plane for?' The master jumper then bumps him out. Don't make John have to do that. Okay? I told him how you are really learning quickly."

She kept up with everything. I eventually found out why. Jenny was a private commercial pilot for one of the largest executive personnel, air transportation companies, and was in layoff for three months, since the economy had slowed. Her schedule was to return to her position as soon as her plane met its FFA requirements.

John showed up every day, but headed to the hangars to oversee that all the mechanical work being done at his business was up to par. There were five other mechanics working with him who never seemed to come in, so that I could meet them. I guess they had heard of my terrible cooking.

One Friday afternoon, John came in and told me to go with him. He drove to pick up Jenny and they both had a surprise for me. I was getting a permit to participate in John's upcoming weekend jump and each jump counted as credit towards my getting a yellow qualification card.

Furthermore, John was footing the price tag on my behalf. I was grateful, but confused. John was certain I belonged with the group and he planned for my being there.

That afternoon, I met with three FAA officials who immediately began testing me on my knowledge concerning qualification for my own yellow card. It seemed simple, because Jenny had already quizzed me repeatedly on the exact issues. In an hour, I signed my own card.

"Now," one FAA instructor told me shaking my hand, "use this knowledge to maintain a strict adherence to the safety rules. Your next five jumps will complete your yellow card requirements. You were excellent in every test and that is very commendable. Good luck."

Afterwards, we all celebrated my passing those expedited tests by having lunch together at Steak & Shake. John told me he and Jenny were going up that very afternoon and I would be his Big George partner for three consecutive jumps at 3,500 feet. On the number two jump, he would hand over the steering line to me. If I succeeded in convincing him I was ready, my fifth jump of faith would be solo.

I began to get nervous, but I thanked them both for believing in my abilities. Jenny kissed my cheek and told me she was proud and John patted me on the back. Then I knew I just had to do it.

"Just relax like Jenny told me you did with her and please don't do any kicking…for obvious reasons…remember, I too, have crouch and leg straps. I can't adjust it up there, if I'm suddenly in a bind. I'd just have to cut you loose," John said chuckling.

That didn't do a thing for me though. Jenny was going to be the pilot and she was all smiles for me. I guess that's why later when she counted off the first, "Five, four, three, two, one, good luck!" I jumped out determined to succeed.

John was very adept in guiding me down and showing me everything he was about to do, except when we got below two hundred fifty feet. Then he had to concentrate and we touched down in his red, white, and blue patriotic chute. He showed me how he packed his chute inside its backpack to make certain it was unworn and correctly folded. Jenny took us up again and I could not wait to experience that feeling. This time, I kept my eyes open from beginning to end. I was ready.

Again the jump was exhilarating and as soon as we repacked our chutes, John removed the tandem jumping Big George harness from me and said, "I know you are ready, Brandon. I'm going to be right out there with you. Remember the 3/12 slope and just keep your leading edge high when you get to two hundred fifty. We're going out at 8,500 this time, so enjoy!"

"You have the AAD to automatically open your chute and the altimeter right there on your thigh. Pick it up and read it before you think you are halfway. You will be higher than your mind tells you. Keep your head and let this time be yours. Are you ready?" he asked.

"Ready," I told him as I took a deep breath and stepped up into John's awaiting de Havilland with Jenny piloting.

Jenny seated inside, kept assuring me that she was going to be waiting for me when I came down. She had a camcorder. Then the next thing I knew I was facing that open doorway alone with the wind in my face.

"You gonna be a What-fo? You want me to give you that shove, Brandon, or you just going to stand there when Jenny says good luck?"

His words fell on my deaf ears, because when Jenny hollered out, "Good luck!" I yelled, " Geronimo!" and stepped off into my blue heaven.

I looked up and John was out about fifty yards to my right side. He kept pointing at his altimeter and for me to look at mine. I was surprised. Jenny had taken us up to nine thousand feet for safety concerns, I guess, and I was then at five thousand feet.

I began to maneuver, ever so slightly, to look downward to see the grassy field below us and aim for it. John sent me an AOK sign and I returned it. Then he descended rather quickly and I saw him hit and begin walking into his chute to collapse it. I was still twenty-five hundred feet up. His trip was successful. Now I wanted to do the same.

I was now my own pilot, alone in the sky, riding on updrafts and swirls. It was quickly becoming effortless, as I just remained balanced under my chute. I practiced landing, by pretending I was coming on two hundred fifty feet and slowed considerably, even though my altimeter read fifteen hundred.

Eventually, I just rode my chute safely down. I even made a complete circle, once, as I watched the tower's windsock and headed into the wind.

John was already on the ground clapping, as was Jenny. She had her camera running, so I wanted my first solo landing to be as softly made as I could. Nevertheless, I alighted upon the grassy field, took two steps, and fell on my behind. I had to run after my chute to collapse it. Then I sat down on the grass looking up into the sky, wanting to return as soon as possible. However, the day's tests were over, I learned, as I walked back feeling like a real airborne trooper.

Jenny handed me my training syllabus and my new personal logbook where I was to log every jump from then on. There were entries of more jumps than I had made written inside there. It was like getting stripes in the service. The more I logged time in the air the better I was expected to become and my rating grew higher.

"Here, Brandon. This is your official A & B yellow card. I signed you off on it as the expert instructor, because you are a natural, little brother. You must make twenty-five more jumps, still, to get full accreditation, normally. However, we will soon finish all those in the next two weekends, maybe ten at a time, who knows. By the time you are at level H, you will be one of us. Here is your official USPA card, sign it, and carry it always. In addition, our best wishes that you have begun this as our best friend...got it? " he said smiling and then put his arm around both Jenny and me.

Overwhelmed by John's generosity and Jenny's devotion to see I knew everything, I hugged them both back.

We went to the canteen where I threw on some big steaks that I had saved for special occasions and soon we dined on my expertise. I was getting to be quite the chef. I had special steaks for special friends.

I learned quickly that they did a super-advanced course on me and that was John's idea, Jenny told me.

Suddenly, John became my older brother type and he wanted to do everything to keep me happy and there at his airport. It was nice to have a good friend, such as him, but daily he kept referring to me as his little brother. I wondered why.

Hours later, Jenny hugged me and said she had to go. That's partly why they had given me that crash course, she said. I was going to miss her company. She wouldn't be coming back soon, but would give me a hoot as she flew over, she laughed.

Her Mooney took off into the southern sky and she was gone. John left on business and I sat alone in the canteen ready to wash dishes. Then things livened up. I received an exciting call from Chewy.

"Hey, Dude, you got to get out here. The profs are great! They let us drink beer whenever we feel like having one. We are off the boats and somewhere west of Omaha, I think. Anyway, I think you'd be thrilled at the big woods we go through. Then there's devilish looking hills that are eroded and bones sticking out…lots of old fossils and real honest to goodness dinosaur poop. They're like pool balls; just as hard, too. Whuzz-up with you, brother?"

"Obviously it's not as exciting here as with you, but I just got my USPA yellow card today."

"What? You got the disease or something?"

"No, it's certification on parachuting. I got this job, remember, here at the airport. The owner took a shine to me. He and a really nice commercial pilot lady taught me in three weeks how to sky dive."

"Hey, man…why didn't you tell me? You gonna sky dive in on top of us? I saw you could get college credit for that. I bet there's no mosquitoes there either. My butt and back have little red marks all over my behind and ankles. They itch crazy-like."

"Sorry about that. It's probably chiggers. Put some extra socks on and calamine lotion. Don't scratch them either…you can get infection. Got any iodine? Dab that on each one. There's a little insect in every red spot squirming around and that makes you itch."

"I've got to try something…hey, these girls are very friendly. I think one likes me."

"Hummm…what happened to Missy?" I asked.

"I don't know…what did happen to her?"

"Hey, got to go. There's a late customer coming in. Be safe, have fun…bye!"

A mechanic, working later than usual, wanted a couple of burgers, fries, and a large strawberry shake. I obliged his request and sat down to talk with him while he ate.

"You must be Brandon, huh? John has been telling us how fast you learned to jump. Pass the ketchup, please…thanks. I have to tell you something though; John did this same thing to another young guy. He thought that other person was his reincarnated brother. Tom, John's younger brother, was killed in a car accident right out there on the highway. He turned left in front of a semi. They think he wasn't paying attention, because there were jumpers coming down and he was watching them as he turned. It was sad."

Now I understood why John was so nice to me, I thought. I just sat listening to Benny tell me about carburetors freezing up on certain old airplane engines, as if he were reviewing his knowledge in his own mind. He left a nice tip and said he enjoyed the food. He also said he would be a more regular for dinner.

At eleven, after I had locked up a clean restaurant, I showered and headed for my cot. I thought about what Benny had told me, additionally, how I wish I were with Chewy on his trip into the deep woods. In two weeks though, no telling where they all might be by then.

Sometime in the middle of the night, I saw my chance to be there. I had two weeks left and I could drive out to Cheyenne, Wyoming. There, I'd have a pilot fly down the Oregon trail route along 26, until we spotted them and I'd take that leap of faith, right down near them. They wouldn't run me off, I was certain. Yes, that would be my plan. I knew I could now do that.

However, how was I going to explain to John my departure? I fell asleep in a much better mood, but wondered if Jenny had landed in Ft. Worth. I missed her already.

John still wanted me up, ready to jump by noon, and came to get me. The weekend was here and the college girls were also in the canteen doing their breakfast servings. It was crowded by noon and business was booming in the canteen. It was hot outside and most wanted lemonade or air conditioning.

Ten very colorful bi-planes flew in from Oshkosh and they all were college age skydivers and stunt pilots. They had come to give their performances at the airfield at John's request.

While in John's hangar, I was putting on my jumpsuit when several of them came inside and introduced themselves as participants in the jumping activities. They asked to see John's big de Havilland that was for sale. Apparently, John was advertising it for sale and they were in need of a larger bird to carry more jumpers.

I heard one say it had its annual only recently and at four hundred thousand dollars, it was a good investment. Boy, were they out of my league! Anyway, they were using it to make their jumps.

Some were my age from the University of Wisconsin. They were all attending sanctioned USPA jumps, while flying around the country on summer break. They were rich kids on a fling, but seemed adult sensible.

By chance, I overheard one girl mention their next stops were near Omaha, Nebraska for their sky diving event next weekend, then on to Casper, Wyoming for a two-day stop. Next, they were hopping over to Walla Walla, Washington at Whitman College and their sanctioned event. They're final engagement was Fort Vancouver. I knew that was near Missy's home and that drew my interest.

John invited them all to join us in a jump or two, which he had previously scheduled and committed to provide the ride. His first takeoff was in just twenty minutes and everyone scurried to prepare their chutes and dawn their jumpsuits.

Then, a siren blew and the airport shut down to any incoming or outgoing traffic for the next four hours. John warmed up his plane's engine and taxied out onto the airstrip. He had twelve, 3,500 feet passes planned with local enthusiasts, he told me. I was going up as much as I could handle, he also mentioned.

I wanted to tell him first of my plan to head out to Oregon, but he was constantly busy with checking his engine's oil and examining the air fuselage for any wear. John was a safety-first flyer and knew his stuff. To my surprise, John handed me a box with a new colorful jumpsuit that he had just bought for me. Now, I was going to have to tell him of my plans somehow, without sounding ungrateful.

"John, I need to talk to you about something that's important to me," I began.

"What? You want to go out to Oregon, huh…that sounds like a great idea to me. Jenny told me about that, and your friend Chewy called the other day from somewhere in Wyoming. He told me to tell you to hurry on out because they were headed into Oregon's deep woods. He told me all about how you dreamed of the wild. I was that way too at your age. Only my wildness was to own a plane and begin jumping out of it. So, what do you need to tell me?"

"That's it in a nutshell."

Stunned by his sudden insight, I could only tell John it was the thought that was always in my plans to try it. John told me he was all for it and said these Oshkosh college kids were headed my way.

Greg Solomon was alone and said he would give me a lift just to have someone to talk with. He had consented to take me with him. John had arranged it that way for me. I felt weak and ashamed, and then shook his hand.

"Thanks for everything and thanks for understanding," I told John.

"Well, if you don't get a move on, you won't be qualified to make your big jump out in Oregon…let's roll. I expect after you get that out of your system, you'll come back time and again. You always can, you know."

"Oh, I'll be back for sure," I spoke to a smiling John.

It was intense at first. Nevertheless, when the girls stepped out into the blue without hesitation, so did I.

I made six jumps and each was more thrilling than the last. By my sixth, I felt at ease and it was old hat. I did not participate in the free falling that some of the kids did. You needed a special license for that. They jumped from nine thousand. All I knew was that at five thousand feet, I owned the air around me in a chute. I was ready for Oregon.

CHAPTER FIVE

I had never ridden directly up front in a two-seater Stearman biplane with the raw wind blowing past my ears. Its seven hundred fifty horsepower Wangle engine was so powerful, Greg, the pilot, could practically make his plane go straight up on takeoff, and that is just what he did. Then he banked hard and did a slow barrel roll down the airfield for John. Of course, I was seat-belted in or I would have splattered all over the runway. We waved good-bye and John waved back. Then he was a speck behind us and the big sky country was before us. It seemed like only minutes until we crossed over the Missouri River and an airfield runway was out front.

"That's Columbus Municipal Airport!" Greg my pilot told me over the intercom screaming. "We'll gas up, get a bite, and hit the hay early. My uncle owns a farm near here. He will pick us up, and we can all spend a few nights camping and fishing at his lake. Saturday, we will be jumping at the field. Can you barbecue?" Greg asked.

"No, but I don't have an aversion to eating some," I chuckled.

"You don't get off that easy. You are now the designated rib man. You'll get help, but these guys can get awfully hungry after an afternoon of air time."

I settled back and watched the nose of the Stearman tilt up to where I could not see the floor anymore. All of the colorful planes had been bobbing up and down on both sides of us, but now Greg's Stearman was out front, flaps down, and that big engine's noise quieted into being a tolerable rumble. Greg set his bird down without as much as a tire squeal. As I looked behind us, the others touched down all in their own graceful way. The planes lined up, then shut down facing west.

"Leave your chute behind your seat. Just tilt it forward and place it behind there. That way, you will not forget it and you will never go up with me without one. There is a FAA certified rigger here. We will rent a chute for you at the hangar's sport shop."

I made three jumps that day from the fifteen hundred levels but felt like I wanted to stay in and go up with the skydivers. My last leap of faith, was on a five thousand feet high whim I made to myself that I was ready to be a freefalling skydiver like them.

After everyone had jumped from the big plane, the pilot always circled high above or left immediately to land. This time he circled high above them and I found myself directly above the group, which had formed a big circle by clasping hands, just prior to their letting go. It would be like an explosion in the air for the crowd below to witness. Without much thought, I decided to leap out and freefall right through the circle they had formed. It was certain to be a hit with the crowd below. I would then deploy after my altimeter reading was 1500 feet. Therefore, as I said, I jumped.

I had never made a freefall like this before and I began to tumble in the air, out of control. Nevertheless, I pushed hard against the air that was rushing against me and quickly regained my air stability with my arms. Quickly, much too quickly, I was approaching my new friends with great expectations of receiving their delight upon them seeing me pass through their big circle. However, I missed hard and as I looked up, I saw startled, angry faces that grimaced at me. I felt sick for doing it.

At fifteen hundred, I yanked the cord and my chute deployed to a happy crowd below. The rest of the divers safely landed near me, one at a time, but they were not impressed. I was told I had endangered everyone's life and they cancelled my trip with them.

"No second chances here, Brandon," Greg advised me frowning. "We thought you were a schooled and a decent guy. However, what you did just then, after you were taught about "joy riding" in classes and forgetting everything you learned about safety, just cost you your card."

"Hand it over," agreed the FAA administrator, who was in attendance and wholeheartedly aligned with the others' sentiments.

I reluctantly gave him my card, went over to Greg's plane, got my chute out, and then headed for the canteen to get something to eat. I wanted to go hide my embarrassment.

As I walked into the restaurant I about died when I saw everyone's faces. There were actually boos from the other skydivers. A second thought, before I leaped might have saved this deserved embarrassment, I imagined. Nevertheless, it was too late now. I found a corner booth to hide and a somewhat polite waitress who tried to ease my pain.

"You're lookin' like the south end of a northbound horse, right now…don't let them get to you. They'll all be gone by suppertime and you can go away to wherever you go and try all over again."

"I don't have a place to go now…that's my biggest problem. I was hitching a ride with them to Oregon to meet up with a friend who's on a college exploration expedition. They're walking along the Oregon Trail by now."

"Shucks, there's nothing but black forests for the most part…lots of bugs and mosquitoes, some pretty little brooks, that's all…why I've flown over that area many times myself."

"You have! Who flew you? Maybe I could hire him to take me over that forest."

"That he, is a she, and that she, is me! Did I just rhyme something there? Humm…anyway, my name's Kitty…Kitty Hawk Carlson… my pop named me that. I also operate a dusting service for that area. I part-time it here, as a cook, a server and a bottle washer on weekends. What's your handle and what do you do?"

"Oh, hi, glad to meet you…my name is Brandon Webb the horse's pa'toot of the day!" I told her. "Why do you fly over that area, may I ask?"

"Tree bugs, mites, fungus and mosquitoes, silly. The US Forestry Service hires me to spray for insects that attack our trees. I get paid by the number of acres I protect. I have a contract."

"And how many acres is that?"

"Give or take a thousand, about three hundred thousand acres of prime deep forests. It seems they cannot afford to get those newer, faster ships inside those deep gorges and then zoom straight up the steep canyon walls. Bugs get there too…I do the dirty work…but I enjoy every minute of it. When I save up enough, I'm buying a French-made

Fulton race plane and entering the money races in Nevada. Right now, I have my dad's old Cessna 188. It's getting its annual right now. "

"Do you ever haul passengers?"

"Nope…who would want to get in a smelly old chemical plane without a gas mask on, do flip-flop banks all day and land on a back country dirt road…who?"

"Me!"

"Okay, I'll fall for your joke…why?"

"It's been my life-long dream to walk inside those forests and feel the solitude that comes from being completely void of humans."

"What? You some kind of hermit-guy, or are you trying to evade the law?"

"Neither…well maybe the hermit part…it's just something I have to do…like your wanting to race planes."

"Oh, yeah…I get ya. Well, if you can stand the smell and can wash dishes and help me clean up around here after ten, I'll give you a hitch-hike over the forest when my plane comes out of the operating room. I'm scheduled to hit the air in three days, if the weather holds like it is now. I guess you want to jump out up there, eh? Where you think you'll land?"

"Well, I never really thought about that, but yes, that's a great idea. I can steer my way down."

"I'd have thought that's just what you had planned."

"Not really…I thought I might have someone land someplace ahead of the expedition and wait for my friend to get there. I had cellular contact with him, but I guess his cell went dead."

"We'll work on those dirty dishes back there in the kitchen and discuss matters after everyone leaves. Jack, my supposed-to-be helper didn't show today, so you're a welcomed sight, believe me."

It was as if I had returned to my old job at the airport because I was washing those plates again. After closing, I swept up the place, while Kitty mopped and wiped the tables. I took out the trash. Then we sat down to talk sipping leftover drinks from emptying the lemonade machine.

"So tell me, please, how does a nice looking girl like you get racing planes in your blood?"

"My pop and brothers are fire bombers."

"You mean they fly into forest fires and drop water on fires?"

"Yep! Mom says Dad was babysitting me when I was almost one and had a scurry call to a blaze to save some ground personnel and took me with him. I guess all the excitement stuck. It was never verified that he actually did take me along, but I kind of remember pooping in my diapers after some kind of herky-jerky up-and-down ride in the air. Dad won't admit to it," Kitty laughed.

We made plans for me to sleep in the visiting mechanic's bunk and Kitty would check on her plane in the morning. Therefore, I slept on a cot and heard all the sparrows fluttering around all night wondering who I was. I didn't sleep much anyway. I kept thinking of how ignorant I had been. I didn't even get to thank Greg for the ride he gave me out to here, before they disgustedly all flew out. I tossed and turned every time I rethought in my dream of my jump and it always came out the same...I missed.

At dawn, the big doors opened and several mechanics strolled inside. They started up a coffee machine and ate donuts they had brought with them. They knew I was there and offered to share their coffee and breakfast donuts with me.

"Kitty called me last night and told me you would be sleeping here on the cot. Was that really you that tried to untie the knot up there yesterday? I hate to say this, but that sure was a dumb stunt you pulled...someone, including you might have been killed."

"I realize that. It doesn't change things to apologize, but I tried."

"Kitty's Cessna is finished. It has to be inspected today and she can go back working on her dusting. The ceiling is good for the next four days."

I nibbled on a donut and walked around Kitty's plane. It smelled rather medicinal, but just like my farmer-uncle's milk cow parlor in his barn. I could stand that smell.

At eight, Kitty walked in wearing an old leather pilot's helmet, which did not do much for her appearance. Her baggy, blue jump suit gave her the appearance of the cookie monster on Sesame Street. I just stared.

"Good morning, co-pilot!" Kitty quipped, as she began walking around her plane, and then stopped.

She lifted the engine hood and pushed around on a few things, and then latched the hood and turned to the mechanic.

"Find anything?"

"Yes, the carburetor needle valve was in need of replacement and I replaced and tightened two rudder cables that apparently drag when you pull up from a dive. They had wear marks. I put them inside a guide to stabilize them. They work free now. Other than those, you are good to go, after the inspection. And speak of the devil, hi, George!"

A jovial man dressed in a white smock came in. The three talked about the plane's maintenance, as they walked around. They physically examined the whole plane, which took over an hour. Soon after the completed inspection, the inspector issued the all clear. Kitty wrote down the work completed this time in her maintenance book and the inspector signed it.

"Hey, Brandon, you want to go get some IHOP, while I head over to the co-op elevator for some dusting chemicals?"

"Sure, I'm a bit hungry. I only ate a donut with the mechanics."

We left in Kitty's pickup truck and stopped at IHOP. After we ate, we went to the local farm elevator to get the ten, five-gallon containers that were marked with a skull and cross bones, which read "poison" all over them.

I loaded the cans in the bed of Kitty's truck as she went inside to sign off for them. When she came out, Kitty handed me a pair of rubber gloves, a mask, and goggles. I was going to pour that stuff into the plane's spray tanks, after we landed in a special place. We returned to the airport and I began my new job.

"Hey…this stuff won't turn me into the Hulk will it? Why is it so green?" I said loading it onto the plane's storage. It held one day's work of three cans.

"Our first ten thousand acres are the aspen. The trees are in full foliage and leaves are bright yellow this time of year. It's impossible to know where the spray is landing looking down, unless there's a coloring added to the spray. On green leaves, well, they shine from the liquid, so nothing need be added. You just have to learn the difference…you will."

"How many of these do I pour into that tank?" I asked

"It mixes with equal amounts of water, but I have to put in this coloring powder, too…one per tank. We'll do that at the landing site."

Just then my cell phone buzzed. Before I could answer it, Kitty grabbed it away.

"Don't you ever turn your cell on anywhere near the fuel or additives!" she scolded. "Here, if she wants you to stay alive, have her call you after work," Kitty warned seeming a bit peculiar.

Then she handed it back to me and told me to take a walk...away from her plane. I just turned it off, stuck it back in my pocket without seeing who called, and began pouring. I hoped I hadn't gotten off on her bad side, so I told her I wasn't going to receive a call from my girlfriend.

"I sometimes get calls that are ridiculous advertisements, but seldom from a girl. I'm not dating anyone. I hoped to receive communication from my roommate to let me know where his expedition is, remember?"

Kitty didn't say anything, however, she smiled, and then told me to get my chute on, if I was flying with her. I slipped it on and looked for a step-up to the front seat.

"Here, put your left hand there on the strut, your right hand on the foam seat cushion and take one big jump up like a pole-vaulter!"

"You're kidding, right?"

"Yep, I just wanted to see someone try that."

Then Kitty pulled out a little step-up and I climbed up easily.

Of course, Kitty tried hard to make me airsick right away when she took off nearly straight up.

Kitty didn't fly very high as she more or less hopped her plane over wooded fence rows and forests. In less than an hour, however, she pulled back on her stick and we rose up very high into the sky. Surprisingly, she turned off the engine in mid-flight and it was super quiet. It was surreal how I could hear her every word.

"You know why I do this?" she questioned me. "I like to listen for nuts and bolts that might rattle around...then I know something's wrong. A wing might be falling off."

"Well, then what happens if you hear a rattle and suspect something is wrong?" I asked.

"Oh, I just jump out and hope for the best. Hear that?"

"No, what!" I thought she was going to jump out right then and leave me stranded.

"That's your heart pounding! Ha!" she teased, as she put that old plane in a stall and then the nose tilted forward and the old bird headed straight down like a roller coaster.

Halfway down in our freefall, the wind was blowing very fast past my ears. When I opened my mouth, the air came in and billowed my cheeks. I held on for the crash as that ground below widened and I could see the end was near. Was this gal mad?

Then, she pulled back on that stick and I thought I was headed through the flooring, but with the softness of a feather, Kitty landed that old plane on a dusty airstrip. I looked back at her and she was grinning from ear to ear. She taxied the plane up to several others which were parked in an open-ended hangar. Several men waved her to shut down and she shut down that engine.

"Dad, Bob, Gene, this here is Brandon Webb. Brandon, meet my folks. Brandon wants to help me out, till I get over by Pioneer Pass. I think he knows Missy. He wants to jump out there."

"Hello, Brandon! See by the look on your face you feel lucky to be alive, huh? I saw Kitty comin' in. She gets mean sometimes. But, you were never in danger. She was testing the wing's ribs for sprayin' like I taught her from up high. Where'd she say you were headed?" her dad asked me with a southern drawl.

"Glad to meet you all…ah, I'm trying to catch up to a college expedition headed up the old Oregon Trail. I just want to see the wild."

Then he slowly and strangely raised his arm and pointed with his finger like a gun to the northwest, "About one hundred miles that way," he tried to align with. "Nothing up there except woodies."

"What are woodies?"

"Oh, if you go out there you'll find that out for yourself. Saw some once. You'll see," was his mysterious reply.

"Brandon…Dad said he saw strange looking people in the woods years ago. He calls them woodies. He tells that story to scare everyone out of there. He thinks it will keep the forest fires down from hikers and campers. He has been known to imbibe in a little lightnin' sometimes. Dad's originally from Tennessee and makes good lightnin' every now and then. I spray it on my garden to kill the ticks and chase lizards."

"Well, that's a good name for someone who lives in a woods all right. But I know when you're joking with me. Do you all have such a fine sense of humor?" I asked.

The guys just turned around on me and went back to working on one of their planes. Kitty tapped me on the shoulder and showed me where to unload the cans of liquid spray.

"Tomorrow, we'll get loaded up and out early while there's no wind…early as we can. I might get you near where you want to be. How do you know the Wrights?"

"I didn't tell you anything about knowing the Wrights. But, I go to college with their daughter."

"Missy? Missy goes to college? Well I'll be darn! The Wrights own everything I don't spray. Their property borders the federal forests and there's where you'll find your woodies, if there are some. The Wrights have the thickest bramble anywhere."

"Are you still trying to tease me? I'm determined to try for it, so I'll hope you let me fill up on water and buy some food from you before we go. I thought there would be a store close by where I took off."

"Nope! But you can have some of our jerky and I'll do you up some lard biscuits tonight to take along in a poke. You can drink the water right out of those streams…just watch your backside for the griz. I see one or two once in a while from the air. They roam all over up there in those woods. Tell the Wrights, Kitty Hawk said hi for me. Might drop in there come harvest cutting time to check if their bugs are a problem. Tell 'em, because I might drum up some business."

Kitty Hawk…everything she spoke about that deep woods was electrifying my adventurous mind. Hardtack jerky and biscuits…just like the pioneers. I was so thrilled by her generosity I just had to kiss Kitty for her helping my dream come true. So after I sat the last can down, I hugged her and kissed her and said, "Thanks!"

"Stop that feller…she's our sister!" Bob yelled out.

"Oh, go back to fartin' around on that old bush plane," Kitty yelled back to him. "You're welcome, and I'm glad to help you, Brandon. You're a good sport and I hope you get your dream."

"I hope you get your dream, also. If I was a betting man, I'd bet you win that Nevada air race someday. It's been fun."

I checked and repacked my chute, while Kitty threw logs in her wood burning cook stove. She took out flour, milk and rendered lard and then commenced to make biscuits and gravy for everyone's supper.

Out back, below their log cabin home, was a pig pen and chickens running around loose galore. Sausages hung on strings in a smokehouse and I saw a real copper coiled still up on the side of a hill. If I didn't know better I'd have sworn I was in the hills of Tennessee. Nobody washed up for supper, they just sat down and commenced to eatin'.

When morning came I was awakened by Kitty. I had slept on a cot outside under their overhang and it was a great sleep, except for a few weird noises coming from animals out in the forest. I got up and Kitty handed me my poke, as she called it.

"Got any more of those smooches? Just for luck?" she asked.

"How can I resist the woman who is going to deliver my dream?"

I kissed her like a man should kiss a woman, hard and meaningful.

After I put on the safety glasses and gloves, I mixed and stirred up the spray, added coloring, then poured it all into the tanks. I also had to hook up the proper hoses. One test squirt by Kitty and we took off in that plane headed for the deep woods.

"When are you going to spray?" I hollered back to Kitty.

"I only spray with the wind on my return. I figured sixty minutes out, then bank, you jump out then and I'll spray all the way back home. It's the safest way to be lighter headed home. Sit back and enjoy the scenery, it's amazing down in the foothills. It will get a lot greener and the trees are going to be two hundred feet high where you'll be jumping. I'll signal, then circle you till you get down. Then I'm out of there, okay?"

I gave Kitty the okay sign and looked below. The amazing yellow aspens had passed us by and now there was a sea of green; we had reached the base of the mountains. Then I heard the engine sputter and I looked back to Kitty.

When she saluted me good-bye, I threw her a kiss. I yelled goodbye to Kitty, as I crawled clumsily over the side and walked cautiously out onto the wing and actually fell off the side, because Kitty dumped me over, clear of the tail, with a barrel roll.

She laughed, and I tumbled out at about fifteen hundred feet. The tree canopy was closed below, with very few openings, but I had no other choice. I aimed for an opening and screamed out.

CHAPTER SIX

"Geronimo!" I counted out a quick five seconds, then I pulled my chute's cord. It billowed almost instantly. I was gliding, headed for the real frontier below.

Kitty circled and waved, then her plane banked away. I saw misty spray being emitted from the bars on her wings and quickly she was gone.

I first saw an opening in the treetop canopy and thought I was in luck, but mountain downwind currents drew me straight down. I had never experienced that before, but I knew I was going too fast when a tree top smacked me across the face.

When I cleared several limbs, I hung up on one and dangled momentarily, until my chute almost collapsed around me, but then I fell fast and it partially reopened. I could barely see, since my eyes were watering. I was headed for rushing waters below. I didn't panic right then, because certainly water was better than hitting the hard ground with a chute not completely opened.

I had come down through the tall trees, headed right into the middle of an ice-cold trout stream's creek bed. I unfortunately landed too swiftly, and was dragged and bounced much too hard against a huge jagged-edged granite boulder. I was bleeding from a big gash on my forearm that I could see and something bad was wrong with my leg covered by my jeans. The pain was excruciating.

Immediately, I lay squirming in the water, screaming out helplessly, feeling broken and dying, until I actually fainted and the lights went out in my brain. My face slipped below the water, but luckily that shockingly frigid stream snapped me wide awake quickly. I was shivering, freezing, and began to suffer from hypothermia. It might be springtime down the mountain below, but it was cold, icy water running up here.

The mountains of the area were receiving the spring sunshine and had begun releasing their melting snow from high above into the streams where the rainbow, cutthroat and brown swam; now me.

Semi-conscious, I let the current carry me to shallower water and got hung up near the shore. The icy overhanging fringes broke away and were sharp as glass, and without gloves, I just slipped off from my hold each time I tried to get up. Then I floated some more, bobbing along like a cork, until I hit a brush pile's logjam.

I became entangled upon a fallen dead tree's limb. That limb kept me from floating further down the stream and unfortunately from dragging myself onto the bank. I was stuck, helplessly pinned there for hours; too weak to shake loose. The pain was torturous, and I feared by sundown I had seen my last sunset. The blood from my hip began to turn the water red around me.

Suddenly, I smelled a horrible stench. That ripe, skunk-ish odor made me fear the worst. Somewhere close by lurked a roaming grizzly. Apparently it had caught my blood's scent and I'd surely be eaten alive; right after he had violently ripped off my limbs, one by one, and wrestled with my body torso's carcass like a toy.

I had seen and heard the "what to do" stories if a hungry bear attacks. Defenseless, no gun, no knife, and a severely broken hip, I knew there was only one thing left. I had to close my eyes and play dead, no matter if the bruin began to chew off one of my appendages.

First I felt a nudge on my head and heard the grunts. Then it was the tugging on my chute, which caused so much body pain that I almost screamed out. I continued playing dead, as I felt the mighty grip on my arm. I was being dragged up out of that ice water. It dropped me onto a grassy ledge and my chute suddenly dropped or was thrown over me.

I thought it was walking away, and when I peeked, I saw the immense body and the long hair. Then, that animal started covering my whole body with the grasses, tree limbs, and leafy bushes, until I was almost buried. It felt a bit warmer then, until it urinated upon me.

I guess he left his scent behind to show other carnivores that I was his meal.

Helpless, I heard it shuffle away through the leaves. The animal left me then, but I knew its return would be at some more convenient time, when he would come back to finish the job. Luckily, I passed out while desperately trying to hold my breath from the animal's terrible urine stench.

During long hours of torture, while still helplessly buried beneath the debris, my entire life flashed before my eyes, in a wondrous, dream-like journey.

I thought of my father's and mother's smiles; my grandparents, some of them that had passed. I thought of Chewy and Jenny and Missy.

Then I thought of Brandon Webb for some reason and realized that was me. I felt myself and I was still alive and breathing. I regained consciousness. I used my hands and started digging my way out of the debris.

My hip was numb, I had stopped bleeding and I wasn't feeling any additional pain. Then I saw it standing right over me like a big cloud. The stench was still there and all that hair left a blurry image. I rubbed my eyes twice, because I knew it wasn't a grizzly. I had no idea what it was, but it sat right down next to me and started grunting and poking me everywhere, until I screamed out. Then, I took a poke back at the hairy monster when it touched my hip. Its hand enveloped mine, but instead of squeezing the life out of me, it stroked my forehead and hair like my mother had in her most gentle way when I was a boy.

"Uhhhhhheeeehuh! Uhhhheeeehuh!" it spoke to me in its own way. Somehow those moaning sounds didn't seem hostile, but I didn't know how to respond. Then I saw other hairy figures and they formed a circle around me. One brought a real gourd of creek water for me to sip saying, "Uhhhheeeehuh!"

I took a sip of the water and that big hand stroked my hair again. Then quietly, another completely surprised me and picked me up ever so gently into its huge hairy arms. He was huge, maybe seven feet tall. I felt like a mouse in a lion's grasp, yet it was tender and without any effort at all. He was very strong. They all turned to walk away, but the hairy animal which held me, cuddled me tenderly, as if I were a baby.

Yeti Brown

It was amazing how quietly everyone walked through the forest. They strode long quiet strides and we moved quickly, but in single file as if a mother hen was leading her chicks. As they walked single file around a bend, I counted there were eleven members. I felt no fear then, as the beast holding me kept patting ever so gently on my bottom, just like a mother did its baby. I think we all traveled for ten minutes very smoothly. Then we started going uphill and I felt more weight upon my injured hip.

When we had traveled ten minutes more, I noticed the gash

showing red through the rip in my jeans, but it had clotted into an ugly mess. Still, we went up and up, around big boulders and suddenly descended into a huge cave formed by an overhanging cliff, high above the creek bed.

I couldn't believe my eyes when I saw the most brightly burning campfire with a ring of rocks circling the burning logs. I felt comforted by how warm it was inside. The glow off the figures' faces showed human-like, except for the hair around everyone's faces, I realized these might be Yeti. Yeti were a long thought extinct group of nomadic ice age people who had apparently come down from the northern-most continents, hundreds and maybe thousands of years ago. They had been found in Asia, but never identified to be as far south on the American continent.

They began to examine my body and grunted little quips to one another, until one looked at the other and ripped open my pants to see my bloody injury. Then one went to my foot and moved my good leg. I showed no pain. Next, when he wiggled the injured leg, I screamed out, and he drew back and stopped.

There were more grunts of their conversation and I could see one was the dominant figure, ordering others to leave and get out to go somewhere. He kept motioning, get out, as to tell them to hurry away. They all left.

Nonetheless, soon one came back being almost too happy, rocking back and forth upon its big feet, as if it were dancing. In its huge hands were long pieces of birch bark, which looked blackened, almost rotted, showing a tarring or gummy-like substance. Apparently, this guy had chewed some of it and liked it, too, because its runny substance dripped from its mouth when it grunted rather jovially. He might have been drunk.

The dominant one scraped off the black gooey mess from that birch bark and rubbed its sticky goo all over my arm's wound. He packed it on and looked me straight in the eyes and gave a short grunt at me, "Uhhhheeeehuh!" I saw he had kind, brown eyes; everyone had brown eyes, mine, too.

Almost immediately, I felt no pain, but then I could tell my leg was limp and probably broken. The dominant one pushed that gooey mess into my mouth and spoke a stern grunt when I grimaced, "Uhhhheeeehuh!"

It tasted bitter-ish, gummy-like, somewhat like the stuff I once stuck in my mouth from a bleeding peach tree, when I was a kid. My grandfather had told me to chew it, because he said it was called frontier gum. After the bitter flavor dissipated, it became like a chewing gum and lasted a long time. I dare not swallow it for fear of dying, nor spit it out which might have angered my grandfather, who had taken his own to chew and was smiling. Soon, I was smiling, too.

I became giddy and felt intoxicated after chewing the dominant one's offering. After awhile, the dominant one moved my sore leg and there was no pain.

Then after a few grunts, the dominant one put its huge arms gently around me and just picked me straight up like a doll and held me out; my legs dangled off the ground and I felt that broken bone shift back down into place, but without pain. I then knew it was trying to straighten the broken bone in my leg…he knew it was broken. I was simply amazed by his wisdom. I guess they, too, dealt with all sorts of injuries and sicknesses.

When the tribe returned with more birch bark and numerous other plants they put water in a hewn out log and dumped everything inside. I couldn't imagine why they were actually mixing everything in mud and even the fire's hot coals. I learned it was all to make a cast for my leg.

Instead of a modern walking plaster cast, I was slowly and gently placed on the bare floor of the cave near the fire, and upon my good side. That mixed up goopy mud was then heaped up and packed onto both legs, so much so, it was up to my navel. I became immobile. It was quite intelligent, I thought, nevertheless I began to worry.

One smoothed out the mud all over me, dripping water on the mud, until it was thick and very slick-looking. I wondered just how long I was going to be inside this contraption and what if I had to go? Then the dominant figure attending to me poked a big hole near my behind. I had my answer, which frightened me. He started laughing again, and everyone else joined in clapping like children for what they had accomplished. They seemed very pleased. I was, too.

"Thank you!" I spoke out to their surprise and they all began to laugh like real human beings. But soon they stopped laughing, and as suddenly as they began, they returned to being serious again. They continued grunting to one another, as if I were not even there. I was left by the fire to dry and that mud cast became hard as rock. I certainly wasn't going to move inside there.

Then a smaller, obviously younger figure walked into the cave dragging my parachute. It put the cloth up to its hairy face and rubbed it. I could tell it thought it was smooth or soft by the way it grunted out its mellow tones. I was beginning to see the tones had everything to do with their communication.

"You may have it!" I spoke softly to the smaller figure and it started a laughter going among them all. I guess they really thought I was a comedian, but the goo in my mouth kept me inebriated. I was feeling no pain.

During the nighttime, I became aware of that skunk-like smell. It had thickened the air inside the cave with stench. All eleven members of the group lay down side-by-side. It was then possible to distinguish the male from the female from obvious appearances. To each his own love must he find and apparently they, too, had their biological urges, taken at their own will openly. I closed my eyes, however no one else there seemed upset.

I felt the need to take a whiz and found myself wetting upon myself inside the cast. I knew I would eventually smell just like my new acquaintances very soon. It wasn't a pleasant thought.

The sunlight coming through the forest branches landed in bright prism streaks upon the floor of the cave. Suddenly, looking around me, I realized that I was completely alone. The eleven had vanished without a sound.

However, I noticed my fire had fresh logs on it and my cast was solid as a rock. It was so heavy, I was expecting now that I would die right there for some future explorer to find, unless a hungry griz came and got me first.

Then, I brushed the mud off my injured arm because it itched unbearably. I was amazed to see that the wound no longer was there. It had vanished, healing so extremely quickly; there was no scab, no scar, just my normal skin and hair as fresh as new. I quickly looked to my other arm thinking I had the wrong arm, but no, that wound was gone. I was thrilled.

Then I noticed a chunk of birch bark lying next to me with some blackberries, a dead frog and a small trout placed on it. There was a small heap of that goo placed there for me, also. I was having breakfast in bed, believe it or not.

I had to stare at it a long time to get the nerve to try it. After an hour, or so, I got enough guts to sample that goo. In ten minutes after I chewed that goo, everything looked scrumptious. In minutes, I pitched the bones from that frog and trout into the fire. I gobbled up the berries for dessert.

One by one the shadow of a figure crossed the cavern's wall before they entered the cave. Each one had some contribution to the group and when the dominant one appeared with a big buck deer, everyone's laugher erupted inside the cave that was almost deafening. I laughed out loud also and everyone stopped to look at me. I was frightened I had spoken the wrong words, so I grunted saying, "I'm sorry!" with my mouth closed. They all began to laugh again. I had found a simple way to communicate with those people…yes, they were people.

I couldn't hear it, it just tickled now and again. I realized my cell phone was on and I was receiving text messages from someone, probably Chewy. I just could not get to the cell. I was healing quickly, but that cast was like steel.

Daily, without so much as one disagreement among them, the Yeti people came and went at their leisure; always with laughter.

About three weeks had passed and I somehow felt the need to hunt, like a dog might, as my nose detected food being brought into the cave's entrance for everyone to share, by one of the eleven. They shared their harvest with me.

One yeti always gathered wild onions and she made it her daily chore to distribute the plant to each of us. I understood when I laughed, she received my thank you. I determined the wild onion sprouts were useful, intended for bowel movements and I was just like the rest. I, too, smelled absolutely horrible locked inside my cocoon-like cast, until I took a dip of that goo, put it between my cheek and gum, and enjoyed where it took me. Only then could I tolerate the world around me, or myself.

One afternoon, when it rained, everyone came back into the cave and there was much chatter concerning me. The dominant one had decided to remove my cast. I thought I had become supper when he rose up with his club and hit the cast so hard, it rocked me and that cast split open.

But, he stopped there from hitting me again and began to drag me under the arms towards the creek below. It was breathtaking to be launched into the icy waters, which had risen considerably.

He joined me in a swirling pool that developed behind a huge boulder and let the water melt the rest of the mud cast away. Soon, the remaining cast released its hold on me and sunk. My legs spread apart naturally then and I was able to swim without pain whatsoever.

The dominant one watched my every move, then grunted to me. I could tell he was asking me what was I doing? He seemed fascinated by my being able to swim and more so when I dove under the water and surfaced again.

He began to laugh that "Uhhhheeeehuh" sound, even had a smile.

That brought everyone to the stream to see me swimming like a fish and they watched me laughing. I dove down, then resurfaced behind a rock to surprise them. They didn't know it, but I was cleaning myself, as best I could without soap. It was an ugly feeling.

Then I remembered my cellular was in my pocket. Surely, it was too long ago, before it had its last charge. Nevertheless, being underwater ruined everything electronic. Everyone knows that.

On the other hand, when I reached inside, I found it was locked in a sandwich bag with a lard biscuit that Kitty had stuck in there to surprise me. The biscuit was flattened and crumbling, but my ultra thin-cell hadn't been disturbed. I returned the bag to my pocket and arose out of the water to greet my friends standing on two sturdy legs.

They all began laughing. I looked where the big gash had been in my hip and it had disappeared, also. Now to me, that was simply world-shaking medicine. I walked over to the dominant one and held out my hand to shake his. He just looked confused at my gesture. He pinched my old wound to see if it was healed, then smiled.

"Uhhhheeeehuh!" I grunted confidently, and he then put his hand on mine. I began moving it up and down, smiling and laughing, and soon I thought he would pull out my arm from its socket, but he stopped when I spoke.

"Uhhhheeeehuh...thank you!"

I thought it unusual to greet someone without using their name, so I named the dominant one Yeti Brown, because of his totally brown hair except for his hands showed some white.

"Uhhhheeeehuh, Yeti Brown," I said, pointing to him.

"Uhhhheeeehuh, Brandon Webb," I said, then pointed to myself.

He looked very sheepishly at me, smiled very peculiarly and spoke, "Uhhhheeeehuh...Boo...bo...we...bo."

I really smiled back...that was close enough for me.

"Uhhhheeeehuh," sounded out in the correct tone, sometimes high pitched in anger, sometimes soft and low in understanding, seemed to mean hello and good-bye, just like the Hawaiian's aloha! He seemed to understand then, but could not repeat the spoken words of thank you, because his lips just couldn't form.

The dominant one shushed me away then, "Uhhhheeeehuh!" like he had done the others when he wanted them to go gather food for everyone.

I knew what he wanted. I was now to earn my keep, or leave. He just turned and walked away. I guess it was left up to me to leave or stay. I wanted to stay. I was living my dream tenfold.

I thought of how best I could serve the community. Looking at the feces stuck to some yeti's hair at their rear ends, I thought about building an old outhouse. It was a very unusual task to think of, however it could also be a health issue. I didn't have tools, just American ingenuity.

I first began working by finding broken off, fallen trees, which were about the same size. They were all birch logs I could handle. When I saw a place away from the cave, where two large boulders sat between two trees and both embedded solidly right next to a huge ravine that fell hundreds of feet, I envisioned a toilet seat. I arranged logs to afford a hole to do their duty. When it was completed the best I could without tools, it was simple, but sturdy and efficient.

Then I went to get Yeti Brown. He followed me to my invention. He knew I was doing something, but was unimpressed by my modern convenience. I could not explain to him what I had made. He stuck his head in the hole and withdrew quickly when he saw he could fall into that deep ravine. He thought it was a big trap, not unlike the Indians of yesterday who trapped the grizzly and elk.

Therefore, embarrassingly, I had to show him. I demonstrated the use of large leaves instead of Charmin, after I gathered sufficient quantity. I sat down and went. Yeti wasn't smiling and simply squatted and did it his way near me on the ground, then covered it up.

I quickly wiped before he took up a huge boulder and trashed my work of art. He scooped up leaves and brush and covered up my invention. My work was for naught.

He stood there like a father scolding his son. By trying to understand him, I think he was trying to hide all evidence of any appearances of his family's activities. I then realized what I had done. I had built an open invitation for anything or anyone to find and maybe kill his family.

"Uhhhh eeee huh…I'm sorry," I said quietly. He just turned and walked away without further ado.

I was not a contributor to the family and I felt very useless. I couldn't think of something else, until I saw my chute being laid upon. I had a brilliant idea.

Using that old college ingenuity, I eased out some of the chute from under the yeti sleeping soundly upon it and ripped off just enough materials to complete my task. I had read about this before in an adventure magazine. Never once had I ever thought I'd have to use it though.

I climbed up on top of a boulder, high above the water and started making a fishing line. There was enough silk threads in the chute to put together a 1,000 pound test line cord onto a makeshift hook.

I designed the hook out of an eyelet of the chute's tie cord. I rubbed it like a grinder against a granite rock, until I had the curvature of a very sharp, but barbless hook. I'd have to be very skillful to land a caught fish, but it was worthy of my efforts.

I bent down a small tree sapling and striped it of its branches. It was only my height, but that's all I could muster without an axe. I didn't see anyone in camp with any weapon or knife, except the dominant one had a club or two.

I worked for several hours from my high up position. All that time I could see big brown trout schooling below me. I didn't have bait, so I dangled the long line beside one stealthy, big trout and set the hook under its big jutting jaw, then snagged him.

By gosh, he fought to get loose, banged himself silly against a rock or two, like I had once, but I pulled him ashore. I took a long green branch and weaved it through the gill plate and secured the fish that way.

Then I continued fishing, until the trout were so scattered from seeing me, that I couldn't get close anymore. Tomorrow would be another day. I broke off some more green limbs to use for cooking the fish over the fire. I needed six. Then I headed home…home, did I say home?

CHAPTER SEVEN

The laughter from them all was loud and long when they returned to our home at the end of the day and saw my offering. I was pushed down to sit next to the dominate one. I wished I could introduce them all to deodorant, but I guess that would come later.

I felt I had reached the pinnacle of my dream, finding these wonderful cave dwellers and nomads. We feasted on the fish, nuts and berries. There was much gas expelled that night. But, I was safe with them and that birch bark goo was extraordinarily helpful.

I walked outside the cave, practically unnoticed…nobody cared anymore where I went. I decided that the huge boulder where I had fished from offered the best chance to test my cell phone, also. Unbelievably, I had immediate results.

"Helloooo!" It was Chewy.

"Chewy, this is Brandon…can you hear me?" I begged.

"Hey, brother…where the heck are you? I received a call from Missy that you had leaped out of a plane up along the Oregon Trail backwoods. We're headed there…"

"Listen up. I'm alive, but my life might depend upon you getting this right the first time. My cell might go out….hello? Hello?" My cell went dead.

I sat there looking at my cell and almost pitched it into the stream, but instead placed it back into its sandwich bag. I almost cried, until I took a pinch of that goo back in the cave. Then I was happy again.

At daylight I had hooked five more fish and hooked a passing beaver by the tail. I yelled out, "Uhhhheeeehuh!" so loudly the dominant one came running.

His eyes were as big as his stomach when he saw that big sixty-pound tree-chomping varmint.

Bonk! The dominate one hit that beaver over the head and that was the end of my struggle to hold it.

Then, Yeti Brown stepped into the stream and grunted several times to get my attention. He slapped his big hand upon the water loudly and it sounded as if it was a beaver tail's smack, just like beavers used to alert other beavers of danger.

Yeti Brown started laughing and I joined him. However, he ruined that beaver pelt, which I thought would be used for some sort of clothing. He was so strong, he ripped the skin and fur right off the beaver, held it by its black flat tail, and then stuck his fingers inside the belly. Then he pulled out the guts and ate them. I about hurled and my "Yuck!" made Yeti Brown frown at me. Then he offered some to me. Now what?

Others had walked up and I gave my share to them. They gobbled everything down.

I had another brainstorm idea. I sat down in the cold stream and felt around for several water worn, sharp granite rocks. I chipped some of them into axe heads and affixed them to sapling pieces with vines from nearby. My intentions were to use them as weapons to hunt with. I handed the first one to Yeti Brown and he looked puzzled. He hit me over the head with it and they all laughed, except me. That was a big surprise.

When I awoke, I saw Yeti Brown throwing those weapons back into the water. He was very wise. He remained superior to everyone as long as no one had an axe to equalize things. So much for that idea. I smeared some goo on my noggin from a distant birch and it eased the pain of my headache, too.

The weeks passed and one day as I was fiddling with the battery of my cell phone, which then drew Yeti Brown's attention, he started laughing and motioned for me to follow him into the cave.

Under a pile of rocks were more cell phones than I had seen in a long time. Some were the old ones that weighed nearly two pounds, but some were recent as maybe five years old. He must have found them out in the woods, lost by hikers or maybe loggers was my first thought.

"Uhhhh eeee huh?" I asked.

Yeti replied with laughter and several grunts. I wasn't making headway. When I reached for one, Yeti grunted, "Uhhhheeeehuh!" loudly. He pushed me away…he was angry. I guess those were his.

Then there was my other brain storm. I acted like a two year old.

"Nah nee nah nee nah nah!" I held up my cell phone and teased him, it was mine. He simply smacked me with his back hand and laughed…I couldn't laugh because I was slowly getting beaten to death by the person who saved me.

But that was then and this was now. I got silly and swiped out and grabbed the newer ones to see if they had batteries. Then I took off running and laughing, because Yeti was very slow. Yeti saw it was a game and came after me.

I'd look at a phone, and if the batteries seemed dead, I'd pitch it back to Yeti and he'd stop chasing me, until he had examined it. This went on and on, until I got down to the last one, mine.

Yeti was getting very perturbed that he couldn't catch me, so I pitched him my cell.

Somehow it buzzed, he looked hard at it and then dropped it. He suddenly ran back to the cave screaming like a baby. I wondered what had happened, until I saw my screen had Chewy's face lit up on it. That scared Yeti?

"Hello?"

"Chewy, where are you?"

"Heck if I know. I was searching with the rest of the group and I got separated."

"Can you tell where you are?" I asked.

"No, but you must be close, because you've been out of my roaming range, until now."

"Maybe you are…listen up, I'm going to holler. Uhhhheeeehuh!" I sang out with everything I had in me.

"What the heck was that?" Chewy screamed over the cell.

"That was me…you are close!" I yelled. "Uhhhheeeehuh! Uhhhheeeehuh! Uhhhheeeehuh!" I screamed out three more times.

"What was that?" Chewy repeated.

"That was me again!" I hollered.

"If that was you, there's five or six of youins running past me in the forest. Oh, God, I think I've seen Big Foot! Or, Big Footsies, cause they keep coming out of the woods running."

"Chewy, just keep coming my way fast. I might have sounded an alert for help. Can you hear this? Chewy!"

"Yes, it's right up this creek. You must be a half mile up that way… here I come, old buddy!"

Then Chewy hung up.

When I looked up, I was mystified by the sight of twenty to thirty yeti persons, including Yeti Brown and my cave family members. They had all come to my call for help, I guess, and they were here to protect and defend.

There was a lot of grunting in discontent, that it was for naught, but as soon as noises came from down the stream, they crouched and listened and watched as if in ambush. It was Chewy.

Now Chewy never went anywhere without conveniences and he held a brightly chromed boom box that any good break-dancer on the streets of Chicago would have envied.

He had it blaring out so loudly on top of one shoulder, it appeared from a distance he had one heck of a huge glittering head. Chewy was a sight to behold for me, but that hip hop music blaring out at 300 decibels was just too much for those yeti. They headed for cover. I headed for Chewy.

"Brother, am I glad to see you!" I said, as I hugged Chewy, who then backed away and said I must have been in the woods too long.

"Wait, let me explain something you won't believe," I begged.

"If it's about all those hairy yahoos running around in the woods, I've got to hear about them! Are they cannibalistic?"

Chewy knew me and believed me when I told him he was safe and about everything else as he grabbed a Snickers from his backpack… "Want one?"

I took it, but thought about my family who probably were hiding in the cave. Then I saw a dozen people ambling up the stream toward us. One was Professor Martin and he called out to Chewy. He answered him. The group made their way up to us, each seemed very happy, and they all sat down near me.

"So we meet again, Mr. Webb."

He was the professor who I had asked about attending the trip, and had told I could not afford to join his expedition.

"Seen anything remarkable yet?"

"You won't believe me if I tell you," I began.

When I finished, the professor was very thrilled, because he could possibly help claim credit for a discovery of these people himself. He would be able to receive a federal grant for another expedition.

He took me aside and made me an offer I could not refuse. He explained that if I would show him the yeti, everyone could video and take pictures and he would be famous. In my weakness, being offered a position with his college group, I told him to sit tight. He agreed to just photograph them from a distance and nothing else to avoid scaring them, as I asked. I summoned Yeti Brown the only way I knew how.

"Uhhhheeeehuh? Uhhhheeeehuh?"

Then I listened. I heard shuffling and I knew it was Yeti Brown.

Suddenly, seeming from nowhere, Yeti Brown stepped towards us from behind the very rock I had collided with falling through the canopy.

"Uhhhheeeehuh...thank you."

Yeti Brown stood there convincingly, looking at everyone closely. Then he panicked when looking closely at Chewy and he stepped back.

"Uhhhheeeehuh...my friend...my friend," I spoke with my arm around Chewy.

Just then, I got a good glance into the contents of Chewy's backpack. There must have been five full boxes of unopened candy bars. I had an idea.

"Chewy, don't let his smell overcome you. He might get insulted," I explained, with my arm still around Chewy. I led him up to a very cautious Yeti Brown.

"Uhhhheeeehuh...ummm good!" I told Yeti Brown. I offered him an unwrapped candy bar from Chewy's stash. Unfortunately, it was a Baby Ruth and everyone knows the pool joke trick done with those. Yeti Brown's face wasn't smiling. I could hear camcorders humming and clicks from cameras behind me.

"Uhhhheeeehuh...ummm!" I smiled, as I bit off a hunk, chewed it and again offered it to Yeti Brown. He took it and immediately liked it.

"Uhhhheeeehuh! Uhhhheeeehuh! Uhhhheeeehuh!" Yeti Brown screamed loudly, which I guess was an "all clear" message for the others.

They came out from everywhere. One had my parachute wrapped around him and one student said, "Look at him!"

There we stood, in the middle of nowhere, eye to eye with primitive creatures, whose ancestry's genealogy dated back into the eighth century of Asia.

Then the professor spoke to his students. "These yeti here, are also known as the Abominable Snowman, a cryptid, which are thought to mostly inhabit the Himylayan regions of Tibet and Nepal. However, they were capable of moving at certain times of need to be able to survive their environment.

"I believe these wise inhabitants' ancestors must have once crossed over the Bering Strait, in small family groups, back when it was frozen solid. Just as the white polar bear migrated southward to become a brown bear and the grizzly, these people have become non-white, basically brown with some of the females showing white belly hair. Their hair was all white then to hide them in the snow, but now they need to hide in the forests. Nature and the warmth of the sun have made them brown like the grizzly, all because their bodies adapted to their surroundings. As they progressed south, they continued to adapt. Thus, their present brownish hair.

"When they roamed the upper Himalayas, they hunted and ate seals and fish, penguins, and migratory birds that they could catch during the ice age; always searching for food and for a warmer climate. They are, of course, nomadic. Here, in Oregon, they have found the animals, the fish and lacto-vegetarian lifestyle to suit their needs and tastes. Evidently, they have liked it here for some time.

"I believe we are the first to ever have found them in a colony this size. We found them together with Chewy and Brandon's guidance. Only I will get the credit and you all will receive your A pluses when we return. This has been a most successful adventure."

To commemorate our intrusion into their lives, I took Chewy's backpack and asked the professor to distribute those candy bars to all who would come forward. I asked the professor to hand out the bars with Chewy and me standing near and he must say, "Uhhhheeeehuh… thank you" to each who accepted. He began with Yeti Brown.

"Uhhhheeeehuh…Yeti Brown, thank you," he told him, with his hand out. Yeti took his hand and then several candy bars and he actually shook it this time. Then Yeti shook mine. Again, I thought I'd lose an arm, so I handed him two more bars to have him stop.

Then the professor and everyone got a surprise of our lives when Yeti Brown motioned us to his home, our cave, to show everyone their conveniences, or lack thereof. The fire was always going because it was so hard to start it, I told everyone. I showed them my mud cast remnants, still stuck hard to the cave's dirt floor. It was a natural cave, not man or animal made. The stench was breathtaking and the kids could stay there no longer and backed out. Yeti Brown seemed a bit ashamed, so I told everyone to laugh hard, as it meant happiness.

When the laughter broke out, one by one from the students, all the yetis joined in and we all couldn't stop laughing at each other. Finally, Yeti Brown acted as if he heard something and with a soft grunt, those yeti filed into the cave. Something wasn't right with him, so I thought we should leave.

"Uhhhheeeehuh…good-bye," I told him, shaking his huge hand. His smile was as bright as I had ever seen. All the yetis began to laugh from inside the cave, as we turned to head down that cold stream. I told everyone to laugh back, and they did. Maybe that's where it was said, "Those who laugh last, laugh loudest."

About an hour away, we stopped to rest and the professor advised us we were very near the property line and a logging road of the huge Wright Tree Plantation. He had contacted them and they were headed our way with trucks to take everyone to their farm. The rendezvous had been arranged by Chewy and Missy. We left the stream and headed west into the forest using GPS coordinates. Three hours later we heard truck engines approaching us coming up a logging road.

After Missy jumped out of that big stake truck, with its benches used to haul lumberjacks, she came running. However, she went straight into Chewy's awaiting arms. I was a bit jealous, until I saw that big diamond ring on her hand.

I congratulated and hugged them both, but asked Chewy how he accomplished that out in the woods. I learned they got very close before school was out for the summer and he proposed over the cell phone three times.

When Missy finally said, "Yes!" he had his jeweler send her the biggest diamond I had ever seen. Actually, no one knew it right then, but for Missy to show up and kiss Chewy, meant the proposal was completed with an "I do". Chewy was full of surprises.

Every hiker was happy to ride for a change and some looked absolutely relieved, especially Chewy. Everyone looked well tanned and in great physical shape, including Chewy, though I knew he still enjoyed his chocolate bars.

Travel was a bit bumpy, but who cared? We whizzed through those deep woods upon dusty roads surprising all types of wild birds and animals, including one big grizzly, gutting an elk's carcass. An air horn was blasted loudly from the window to scare it away. I guess that was to scare the bruin to make it leery of trucks and humans for the loggers' safety. We eventually arrived in front of the sawmill and huge piles of birch bark chips that were being blown into the box trailer of a semi. They were about to be shipped out, Missy explained.

We toured the Wright's tree plantation for a day. Mr. Wright was surprised when I scraped a portion of the dark goo off the birch bark, which he assured everyone was used medicinally by laboratories to develop medicines. I knew of other uses firsthand. I put a little pinch between my cheek and gum and sucked it like a lollipop. I winked at the curious professor, and then gave him a plug, too. Soon everyone joined in and we were all a very happy group. With everyone giggling, it reminded me of those back in the deep woods.

The professor and I both decided we were going to return as soon as we were better equipped to stay a while. He wanted to try jumping like I did and I had a long story to tell him about that. I had spent three months being a true explorer before I returned to college.

In the meantime, the professor went before the archeological body and gave the speech I wanted to give. First, he showed only the film of himself and Yeti Brown together. But what the heck, I was fulfilling my dreams, getting paid, and I was going back there again.

I stood by his side, after being introduced as Assistant Professor Brandon Webb, and listened to the professor speak to the gathered.

"Today, I want to tell you about an adventure of a lifetime; one you're never going to believe!"

THE HOOTENANNY MASSACRES!

PREFACE

My name is Brad Anderson and do I have a weird story for you!

In the summer of 1956, on June 3, a small group of Boy Scouts, aged 8-14 years old, gathered with responsible adults at their local church hall, in their southern Illinois town of Foster Pond. The boys and some of their chaperoning fathers made preparation for a church-sponsored, overnight campout. Each had packed his own food, own sleeping bag, and his other camping equipment necessities, including some with their fishing poles to use along the creek.

The adult-sponsored occasion was for everyone to take a short, overnight trip from their town, hiking out only five miles into the outlying countryside. It seemed pretty safe and every boy had his parents' permission slip signed and turned in to the scout leaders.

Their pre-chosen campsite was to be on the private property of one generous congregation member and local farmer named Judd Parker, who had accumulated several thousand acres, some which lay along a creek tributary that he had purchased at auction. This secluded area was far away from everything and seemed a great adventure to the boys. It was as if this event was going to be like the utopian trip for young scouts to learn from the outdoor experiences.

On some of those auctioned parcels however, stood old farm houses, long vacated and in various states of deterioration. All were supposed to be inhabitable and for many years they stood unattended and falling apart.

The annual campout event was a reward from parishioners for those boys who had shown up for Sunday school and church for the entire year without missing. No girls ever wanted to go on this kind of trip. The girls of the church in turn went by bus with their mothers to the St. Louis Zoo. It was the most excitement of the year for them all.

Their schedule was to camp out for just one Friday night and march home after a noon lunch, provided by the church sponsors. Nevertheless, when the party failed to return on Saturday, worried parents drove out to the encampment.

Upon arrival, they found blood and destruction everywhere, but there were no scouts or their fathers. Their camp was found in complete ruin. The scene was horrendous and no one could understand what had occurred so vastly.

Their blood-splattered, previously pegged down tents, had been uprooted and were seen strewn out all over the place. Those surplus tents had huge gaping tears in them, and lay scattered about in all directions, as if a wolf pack had dragged them and chewed them up into smithereens.

However, wolves were long thought extinct then and there were no wolf tracks present. Whatever happened out there remained a mystery for years and years, because science and forensics hadn't existed as it does today.

There was much speculation, too, when no animal hairs were discovered, which added to the anonymity of the perpetrator's true being. Was it an animal or human, or celestial monsters? Some feared it was the work of a stray grizzly bear, which shredded the army surplus tents as if they were paper-made. No bears of any kind had been reported in over a hundred years. Confusion led to more speculation and misinformation leading to fictitiously-told tall tales.

Others suggested an undiscovered ancient being like the Sasquatch or Big Foot, even a Werewolf. Eventually, the horror stories that evolved through countless repetitions over the years were lumped together.

That first summer passed without any trace of the missing. It was as though aliens had dropped down and swooped them up into their spaceship; there were no answerable facts. That was the closing discernment in a mass coroner's inquest, held three months later. The final finding on the death certificates was concluded as an "unknown happening".

There were no bodies ever found that might have closure for the involved families' losses. Only eulogies and flowers were there for the funerals. Left with only distant memories, a sermon from an assistant preacher was given on behalf of the missing. It seems their real preacher was an assistant scout leader. The whole town had attended the affair, seated in the only place capable of holding the townspeople and the press, the city's ballpark stadium.

Faithful parents and relatives gathered in hope that their combined humble prayers would somehow ease their pain, so they offered prayers and hoped their massed strength together would somehow return their children.

However, never so much as a tiny clue came from above to tell them that their children were still alive and safe. Eventually, over many years of finding nothing, they gave up hoping and praying one at a time.

Nevertheless, future town meetings lacking agendas, somehow always discussed the incident with much banter. Eventually, time healed most everyone's wounds and after so long the new people replaced the past. Therefore, the terrible mystery was almost forgotten.

In addition, although there was much evidence of violent mayhem, with lots of blood splattered everywhere, nothing much else was discovered there at the campsite, except a noted charred comic book. It had lain too near their campfire and was partially burned.

Its title "The Hootenanny" was still visible; therefore, without much thought, the investigating sheriff's department attached "Hootenanny" to their case, for want of another case marker.

Hence, the case eventually became known as the Hootenanny Massacres. It took fifty years of aching to forget the occurrence; then there came a stirring news headline event; a child was missing.

CHAPTER ONE

At the end of my second semester of my junior year, while attending Southern Illinois University in Carbondale, Illinois, my professor in journalism class gave me a special assignment. This assignment was given special attention because the case was dear to the professor's heart. He had lost relatives in that massacre.

The account that I was to gather information upon, was to be completed at my leisure, but before returning for the first semester of my senior year. He gave me numerous newspaper findings of a rather hideous recount of a group of Southern Illinoisans who disappeared on a camping trip. I was to rewrite the event after I researched its location.

My job was to report to him, by locating any persons who recalled the event, then voice record their thoughts of what they believed transpired. It seemed like a simple task, interviews I thought, although I had to do it with gusto, because it would be part of my thesis later upon seeking my masters. He told me I could develop an interconnected story from people still living in the small Midwest town.

"Oh, yes, it was well supervised. It was not as though there needed to be older persons to chaperone kids twelve and under back then. All of the victims were supposedly very good Christian boys, totally trustworthy," Professor Morley told me.

I learned that there were only thirteen in the group, which consisted of nine boys, three parent adults, plus their preacher. The kids were all thrilled just to hike out with their camping gear. They each brought along enough food for an evening's meal, mainly a couple of glass bottled sodas or Kool Aid, with a few hot dogs and marshmallows.

For breakfast, they brought mostly eggs and bacon to be cooked over their campfire. The preacher had volunteered to help them learn to cook camp meals as he had been an army cook.

Everyone was excited, as they lined up in single file and stepped off marching away at 3:00pm that Friday afternoon. It would take a little more than one hour for their arrival. They planned to be set up by dusk.

Someone kept repeating a "hut, two, three, four" cadence, until it was too annoying to stop and wait for one of the younger stragglers who continually broke stride to adjust his load.

They all marched down a country road to a pre-arranged campsite, which was along the ever-winding Richland Creek. It was new to them all. One parent was also their grade school teacher, Principal Douglas Weber. That was the extent I soon learned, after I sat down and read the leading newspaper articles, which my professor had given me to start my journey.

Chapter Two

I had to envision this assignment must take the investigative avenue, just as a police detective of the current time would begin his investigation. Therefore, I went to the sheriff of the county and asked for advice and help. Their understaffed personnel left me with only their old radio dispatcher, who himself found it very painful to dig up the past. He had lost a younger cousin.

Henry Holcombe was seventy-two, much too old for police work, but certainly still capable of answering police telephone calls for assistance and assigning the proper patrol car to investigate a situation. He had been on the force for fifty years; once an elected sheriff himself, but always dedicated to public service. He was very helpful.

I spent one midnight shift with Henry Holcombe, a part-time police dispatcher, when he told me he had lots of time and the coffee pot was hot and always full. He was the jailer, the secretary's assistant and the janitor, if that was needed also.

Henry got around very well for a man of his age. He wore a retired model 10 Smith & Wesson .38 revolver off his personal belt, which seemed archaic in the days of automatic pistols. Yet, he was as efficient as any on the force.

"I recall the event," Henry began, when I asked him to tell me as much as he remembered. "As I recall, I had just completed my first year and was promoted to west county patrol, which was the worst patrol a deputy could be assigned, because it was the "chickens and the owls" patrol. The calls I got were seldom very exciting and being young and adventurous, I wanted action," he said, with a gleam in his eyes.

Henry told me his "best recollection", as he always began a sentence, was that he once thought himself to be a very good detective. Nevertheless, being so young and inexperienced then, during the massacre, the sheriff of the time, Fess Border, quashed some of his evidence found near the scene. He did it because his department had no money to continue the investigation and forensics had just begun. Certainly DNA did not exist as we know it today as being very important.

I learned even the insane were released back into the public as no facilities were available for help then and the costs were curbed by financial woes of each elected sheriff who had to prove efficiency in his department or lose his job. Out the cell door they walked, unaided, sometimes violent men…frequently insane persons were sent packing.

"As I recall, usually I'd have to take the crazy person across the county line, dump him off, give him my own dollar or two to eat something at a restaurant and let the neighboring sheriff worry about him," Henry advised. "It wasn't good, but that's the way it was. Anyways, we'd received their county troubles back here in our own county, sooner or later. Back and forth, back and forth…always…they got housed for a while when they got picked up, until they kilt someone or kilt themselves."

"What about that massacre?" I questioned.

"I was a'gittin' to that, sonny…it was during that investigation that we all were called to the scene. I found barefooted prints of two people walking away from the scene several days after the scene had been gone over by the state investigators, too. As I recall the sheriff didn't think it was important since he had let so many people make tracks around the scene and even the state boys were angry. You know, the sheriff who didn't get all the press he could get didn't get reelected."

"And?"

Henry took a sip of his coffee, just as a patrol officer called in to headquarters that he was stopping to have coffee at the Hen House Restaurant.

"Ten-four, 88!" he answered him. "Look, I can't start up something that is nearly fifty years old," he turned back to me saying.

"You won't, I will. That's my assignment. Now, what was it you found?" I inquired moving in closer as the police scanners became noisy with a car chase in progress in an adjacent county. He turned it down, because they were a hundred miles away.

"As I recall, I found a little girl's doll and some muddy shoes about a hundred yards away from that horrible scene. There weren't any blood stains nor were they torn either. There weren't no girls along on that hikin' trip neither, so sheriff tells me to forget it. But I didn't…I threw it in an IGA grocery evidence bag anyways and put it in with the rest. Thing is I don't know what happened with the rest."

"What, the rest of that evidence?"

"As I recall, it went to the state attorney's evidence vault. But our old court house was knocked down and rebuilt twenty years ago. I guess it got pitched like all the cases that were unsolved."

"There go my sources," I was reluctant to admit.

"Now wait a second…as I recall, now, I took that evidence back, because I was first on that case and put it all in my attic. It wasn't in the state attorney's office. I wonder if it's still up there. Haven't been able to climb up or down, since this arthritis set in."

"Could you check up there for me?"

"You mean, Brad, can you check up there for you?" he snorted. "I don't intend to go up there ever again. They blew in that insulation stuff up there ten years ago and it might be buried under that stuff…I don't know. But, we'll take a peek anyway when I get off in the morning. In the meantime, that chase just crossed our county line and they didn't notify us. Stand by…Randolph County car in pursuit, this is Monroe County…do you need our assistance?" Henry asked.

"Now I do, Henry, that car just smacked into a big oak on Bluff Road north of Roacher and it looks as if you can call me an ambulance, and get your coroner up, too."

"This is car 88, county…I overheard the call, I'm enroute," the deputy answered without being called out and without hesitation.

I heard his siren in the background, as he called in his location.

"That'll teach you to take a coffee break when mine is better in here anyways," Henry told him laughing.

"Yeah, but you don't look half as good as that new waitress does," he quipped, then went on his way.

As Henry answered the continuous calls about the crash, I looked at the bulletin board for wanted persons. There was a huge display of pictures of wanted criminals, also missing persons. When I noticed a missing sixteen year old girl from Monroe County I examined the info. Apparently, she went missing after her school's homecoming dance.

The poster was just from the past two months, so I asked Henry about her. He didn't know much, except he thought she had a boyfriend and he disappeared, also, on the same night after a school function.

I looked forward and found another missing sixteen year old named Tom Brandson that had his synopsis also. No foul play expected, however it wasn't updated at all. I pulled both from the display as they weren't getting much look-see there and asked Henry if I could borrow them. He got up and put them both on the scanner and gave me copies.

"Would these two be from this area?" I asked knowing they were.

"Yeah, we get kids running away to get married or to try to get abortions in another state. Don't know much about those two. Hadn't any trouble with either that I know of."

Just then several day deputies walked in and got coffee before heading out and they asked Henry about what was happening in the county.

"It's as peaceful as Afghanistan," he laughed. "Who's the new night shift waitress that has Elton stopping in every couple of hours for coffee lately," he questioned them.

Without an answer, the two looked at each other and simultaneously spoke, "That's the girl!" and the two young deputies put down their coffees and hurriedly left. In two minutes they signed off at the Hen House.

"Young bucks…all they do is chase young women…wish they chased criminals that hard," Henry chuckled. "Watch this," he hinted. "Go ahead Unit one," he spoke loudly over the main radio channel, expecting the young officers to overhear his call on their portable radio packs, and then become edgy that the sheriff was near. They were supposed to be riding patrol.

"Unit One is Sheriff Fischer…he's out, off duty, hee, hee…but they don't know it. But I'm certain they heard me."

Both young deputies came back on the air quickly, but nonchalantly. One asked if there was any traffic for them from the sheriff. I, too, started laughing at Henry's prank.

"Nope, sheriff's in church mass till ten. You boys ought to join him," he snickered. "Anyways, it works every time," Henry said laughing.

"Let's go home. I have to feed my dogs or they'll start howling and disturb my neighbors," he continued. "Just follow me home."

I watched the changing of the guard as a lady replaced Henry at the radio counsels and commended him that he had typed up everything for her. And, there was a fresh pot of coffee brewing for everyone's enjoyment, too.

Henry must have typed before I got there. He left at eight, so I followed him as he drove out to a small country subdivision. I heard howling dogs greet Henry's arrival.

He stopped before entering the garage and told me I had to pull down the garage attic ladder to get up there to get the old evidence bags. It was dark, but Henry flipped on an attic light. I saw lots of dusty boxes, some with yellow tape marking them as police evidence.

"Sir, there's at least ten boxes up here. Do you remember which is which?"

"Darn, that is where they all went. I remember now. Yep, it's the smallest one with Deputy Henry Holcombe's writing on the receipt."

I found it and climbed down the ladder. It was very dusty, I mentioned, but Henry was already out back behind the house feeding his canines.

There were two old red plot hounds sniffing him and wanting their food. Henry said the dogs were at least twelve years old and had been his own investment when he was sheriff, ten years back, and had used them both for tracking humans. They looked healthy and well cared for.

After Henry hugged and fed his dogs, he asked me to join him for breakfast. He was frying bacon and eggs and appreciated my company. His home was very nice, very clean, and I mentioned that to him.

"Polly, my daughter, comes twice a week to check on me. My wife passed away almost fifteen years ago and I've been batchin' it since. Marge was a wonderful girl. I just can't find anyone else to like, so… well…how many eggs?"

"You miss her, huh? I'll take two over-easy, if that's fine with you. I appreciate this, since I haven't noticed a motel or hotel anywhere near this town where I can rent a room for a week or two."

"No, and you won't…not for twenty miles. But also don't go feeling mushy about me being an old widowed, lonely bachelor. I have my dogs, my job, and my health is good. I just needed someone to wash all these dishes I left the last two days. I hate washing dishes, don't you? I'm thinkin' a person would be grateful to wash dishes for his breakfast!" Henry chuckled.

"You're right...I'll cook too, if that helps. I see you're limping...is that from sitting all night in that chair?"

"Nah, caught a bullet in the hip at a Coxiville holdup. Some young punks were robbing the gas station, just as I stopped in for gas. They got scared and one shot me."

"Did you shoot back and kill them?"

"Nah, one I recognized as my nephew...my brother's kid. He hung himself later that day when he found out it was me who he shot. I knew he wouldn't have shot me if he knew it was his uncle. His buddy is still in the pen for armed robbery. He shot at me, also, but I winged him. He stood trial."

We breakfasted on my best made scrambled eggs. Afterwards, I also did the dishes. Henry volunteered his "recalled knowledge" of the incident during all that time; I listened, as I washed and dried the dishes.

Then, I took out my notepad, sat down with him at the kitchen table and scribbled notes every time he had a hidden clue. When I asked him about the crazy people back then that he mentioned earlier, his face turned white as a sheet.

"What's wrong?" I quickly asked, thinking he was ill.

"You know...it just first dawned on me, right now, about the crazies we knew were getting state financial aid help. That place was out in the back of a farmer's home back then, no more than two miles from that massacre scene through the fields...where they stayed...well, it was a summer kitchen where they canned and made candles. They put beds in there, too. The first people that owned the farm took care of them crazies until they themselves passed...but I don't remember when. What the heck was their name? It was the same as Fess's mother's side... ah...darn it! Elmer Parker bought that farm later.

"The Hooleys! That was their name...the whole darn family was nuts...I brought several of them boys in two or three different times for stealing polts and even a porker or two, now and again.

"Old Sheriff Border always kept them in jail overnight, fed them real good and made them promise to behave...then he'd cut them loose in the morning. He just up and died here about six months ago. I was a pallbearer at his funeral.

"Anyways, back then they suddenly just quit coming into town…I bet they had something to do with it all this time. I feel sick. No wonder old Fess stopped me from following those double tracks. It must have been that band of Hooley loonies. I'm sick. I'm sick as a dog!" he complained.

"My cooking?"

"Heavens, no, now I have a real honest to goodness idea about who actually committed that terrible massacre. It had to be those Hooleys, had to be. As a matter of fact, I learned later one crazy Hooley was the old sheriff's sister and one his mother. They said he was always ashamed of them and never was seen visiting them. But I once saw them at the back door of his office begging for food. Oh, my gosh!"

That was my first big break, and so soon, but Henry continued to pout about his ignorance of back then. Using my best judgment, I told Henry he could rectify the situation and still come out of it as a real detective's detective. I would help him, since he had a bad hip and together we could solve the crime.

Unfortunately, back at that time of the massacre, the coroner ruled the occurrence, for its lack of habeas corpus, was an "unknown happening". Therefore, no warrants could be received without probable cause. That was my job, and I planned to solve that crime and get my A+ grade, also.

Henry asked me to stay with him and then got out an old portable radio and put a charge into it. He said that I could converse with him when he was on night duty being the county dispatcher.

Then Henry grew very sleepy and slept the rest of the day. I couldn't, so I drove my Camaro into town to the barber shop, hoping to get a haircut and directions to the farm place in question. I thought I would have had no problem, as the town barber always had all the knowledge anyone could use, gathered from his clients throughout the years. Surprisingly, at first he was very reluctant to give me any directions, and only told me how to get there, after a patron voluntarily began to tell me how to get there anyway.

I drove down the bumpy, dirt road, which had so many pot holes my teeth began to chatter. I could see faces peeking out my way through windows, but they all disappeared from sight, before I drove up to the farmhouse. I got out, honked my horn, and then hollered, "Is anybody home? Helloooo!" But there was no answer.

When I knocked hard upon the farmhouse door, I heard feet shuffling, but still no person answered my knocking. I stepped down to go to the rear and saw that there were people moving around in the rear summer house, also, so I went there. Again, there was a quiet. I decided to have a look around, then maybe by my investigative snooping they would get disturbed and confront me. I was right.

I turned the corner of what appeared to be an old summer kitchen home. It looked to have been neglected for many years. The house had no gutters, lacked being painted, and some windows were broken out, covered by torn bed sheets. As I looked around the farm yard it was getting very creepy. I saw no animals anywhere, but I heard strange animal sounds coming from within the house. I whirled around when the front door slowly creaked open and a wild-haired woman's face appeared from behind with a haunting smile. Boy, was she creepy-looking and appeared to have blood on her lips.

The hair actually stood up on the back of my neck. Her face chilled my spine and I knew she was old, scary and offended by my persistence. She held a huge meat clever beside her, as others, young males and females, who were looking as horrifying as she was, came around from the back of her to peek at me.

They quickly surrounded me before I could speak. Someone from behind me smothered me by forcing a canvas bag over my head. I was rolled up and tied inside that thing unable to breathe. I was carried, then dropped someplace dark and damp and left alone. I heard water dripping and possibly a frog croaking. I thought I was thrown in a swamp, but it turned out to be an old outhouse crapper.

I must have laid there for almost a day, until the wetness seeping through the canvas's holes allowed the ropes that they tied me up with to loosen enough for me to move. I inched and inched to get my one hand around the portable radio. It took a while, but I figured out how to turn it on and it squealed sharply. I had my finger on the talk button, so I whispered, "If you can hear me, Henry, I'm at that place and they've caught me. Help!"

Someone then hit me on my head and I blacked out. Again, when I awoke later, I felt alone. However, I soon found out my radio's battery was dead because I had not turned it off.

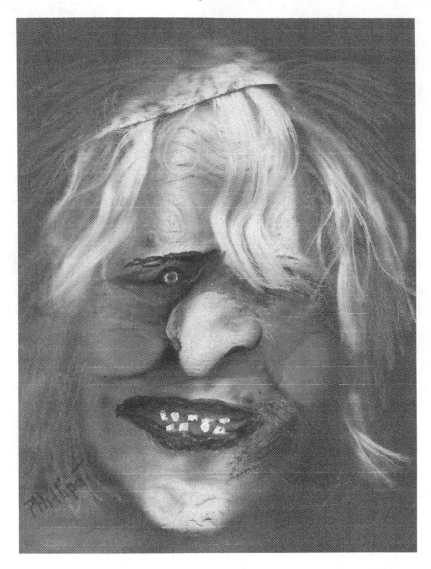

I began chewing a hole in the tarp with my teeth to try to see out of it, until I heard the most terrifying woman's sheiks imaginable. It was torturous sounding and whoever it was, was being inflicted with terrible pains, time and again. Then it was quiet for another few hours. My body was wet and the stench of it began to nauseate me, until I puked up inside the tarp. Now, it was worse…I was lying in my own vomit. I passed out again.

I always was a restless sleeper, my mom once told me. I had this twitching foot action where no one could sleep in my bed with me, unless they wanted to be scratched by my toenails, she said.

Evidently, I still did that thing in my sleep and when I awoke, that tarp was open at my feet. I had cut through the old wash line rope that bound me. I wiggled like a larva in a cocoon, until I was completely free.

Nevertheless, when I discovered they had thrown me down an old outhouse crapper and I was up to my chest, about to sink under in human feces, it was distressing. I clawed my way up and finally grabbed hold of the inside of the hole, then chinned myself up.

Though it was small, my slick, human feces-greased body slid easily through that hole. I peeked outside the moon crest in the door and it was nighttime.

I ran like heck down the road from which I came, until I heard shouts coming from those people from whom I had escaped. The sweat from my upper lip eased down into my mouth and I hurled. I had to rid myself of this crap fast. When I came upon a one lane creek bridge, I just dove straight in to wash off.

After the initial shock of my head hitting a rock, I didn't care much about the stench on me…moreover it was the fresh blood streaming from my head that worried me mostly.

I could not feel of the wound for fear of causing dangerous viruses to enter, so I doggie paddled to the deeper parts and washed upstream, until at last I could feel my skin. My clothes were still covered.

I eased up onto a very sloppy-muddy bank and swirled myself in the mucky, gumbo, goo, until I was virtually a mud ball. It covered the porta-potty smell. I heard voices.

When a flashlight beam's glare blinded me, all I could do was sit still, until it passed me by. Maybe I should have leaped up, made hideous noises and chased them back. I had to look as hideous as they did. But they might have had weapons.

At dawn, I found myself walking along a dusty road headed back to town. Then, a car that was leaving dust swirls behind it, approached at a fast pace. Thank goodness it was Henry. He stopped quizzically, and drew his .38 special to get the drop on me, the mud man. He was lying across the fender of his car, when I asked him if he liked my eggs.

"Advance and identify!" he screamed out to me.

"Thank goodness it's you, Henry. It's me, Brad Anderson."

"For gosh sakes! I almost shot you, Brad. Johnson came in off the night shift and said he heard whispering on his radio. He thought I was playing a joke. He said someone whispered 'they caught me at that place'. I suddenly realized it might be you. Sorry I took so long...how did you get free?"

"Let's get away from this place first. I'll tell you all about it after we get home."

"Where are you going?"

"Oh, don't make me tell you now, but I'm riding in the trunk, so take it easy," I said, motioning for him to pop the trunk. "I didn't get this muddy on purpose for nothing, believe me."

Henry allowed me to ride in his trunk. When we got to his home, I asked him to hose me down well out in his yard. After I felt cleaner, I asked Henry could I then use his shower.

"Sure, you look horrible," he added.

Henry hit me with his best shot and in minutes I was much cleaner. I took a long, soapy shower and came out to an anxiously awaiting Henry. After I told him everything, he grimaced and didn't want lunch...me neither.

That night I rode to work with Henry. We decided to include Sheriff Clyde Fischer, since he was the boss. In the morning I told him everything.

CHAPTER THREE

"Did you have permission to trespass? No! Are you a sworn law enforcement officer? No! Was there a crime committed against you? Maybe, but certainly not substantial enough, without even seeing the perpetrators or without an eye witness. Did you see who did that to you? No. Do you have a shot in getting a search warrant? No! You should have come to me first, young man. I'm surprised at you, Henry, for going along with this shenanigan," were the sheriff's words to us, which made me feel ignorant. He took a deep breath and spoke again, this time more civilly.

"I do admire your courage, son, but a cop has to have developed a strong case of probable cause or the guilty party goes free...and once you make your accusations and bring charges, they get set free if you can't prove your case in court. Then they can't be charged again. That's called the protection of double jeopardy.

"It's just not hot enough to prosecute yet. I don't have the manpower to reopen a case that's fifty years old, although it needs to be solved. I wasn't even alive then and vaguely recall people even discussing it. But it did happen and a heinous crime apparently was committed...and, as far as I know, all the evidence has been destroyed."

"No, sheriff, it has not," Henry rose up to speak to his boss. "Here's one of the evidence boxes I personally did up. I took all the rest of the sealed evidence from that case and placed it in my attic. I took 'em when the circuit clerk was going to burn up all the evidence and paperwork to the unsolved cases that were over twenty-five years old to make room. Heck, I forgot they were even up there, if it weren't for Brad here jarring my mind. I'm seventy-two and I can't remember what I even had for breakfast these days. But Brad here, he's a real go-getter, sheriff, and I imagine if you special-deputize him he can help get this case going again, maybe even solved."

"Henry, you underestimate yourself. I chose you because you're honest and a good man on the night desk…remember that. Now, Brad, I want you to take all that evidence to the crime lab and get a receipt. Don't open anything. There might be DNA or something science can discover that they couldn't back then.

"Brad, raise your right hand. Do you solemnly swear to uphold the laws of these United States, and the laws and constitution of the State of Illinois? If you will, say, I will," spoke the sheriff.

"I will," I answered.

"You are my first and only special deputy. Here's a star to put in your wallet. Don't go flashing it around and don't go arresting anyone, unless your life depends upon it and you've talked to me. You now have the power of arrest, but without proper training, I can't allow you to carry a gun…understand?"

"Yes, sir…and thank you for allowing me to serve. I think I thought somehow you would throw me out of your office. I'm glad I came to you. There is one thing…my car. When I got loose, I left my car behind."

"That, son, was brilliant. If they trash it, we can file charges. But if we see them driving it, and they can't be lawfully licensed, we have an open invitation to print them and interview them. Might break open that case if anyone consents to talk about it. Always obey the laws of evidence and arrest and you'll find the law is written to get the true offender.

"Now…go back to Henry's attic and gather up all the evidence and let's get that evidence to the lab and stay with it until you know what's all in there. If there's blood, it's still researchable, especially if there were bodies buried out there. It might take a while, and after fifty years the perps even might be dead and we're dealing with their ancestors. At least justice will eventually have been served here. Now go with the evidence, Brad. Henry, you best go, too, and show him how to get there. It's in Fairview, but they keep moving it all the time. Keep me informed, deputies."

We left the jail in Henry's car and I climbed back up in his attic to retrieve all the dusty boxes of evidence.

"Your Sheriff Fischer is a very smart man. I sure didn't plan on any of this, but just think what I'll be able to tell my grandkids."

"Yeah, if you make it out alive again," was Henry's chilling response.

The evidence was still intact, carefully unfolded, and examined by forensic personnel. I was receipted for all the items. There were bloody clothes of the time, US Army sleeping bags, Boy Scout backpacks with blood splatters that had turned brown, bloody canvas tent patches and bloody personal toiletries of the victims, plus some solidified, moldy food and unopened fruit cans.

There were two separate pair of barefoot print casts, which Henry suddenly remembered making at the other side of the creek from the tracks he had found. Two were large feet; two very small.

Then I saw that colorful comic book about the Hootenanny. It was charred from a fire. The date on it was June, 1953. It must have been purchased by the victim to be read just before the trip took place.

The five big boxes held much, but was it all worth its weight in evidence? It was as if I was taking a trip back in time.

Henry was given the night off for helping me with that evidence, his first since he started on nightshift, seven years prior. Back at his home, we decided to sneak out to that place again, this time from the scene of the horrible massacre, and take some pictures with his old departmental camera.

The first thing I thought of was to inform the sheriff of our plans, but he was out and the deskman took everything down.

"You boys better wait for the sheriff," he advised.

"We have his go ahead order," I told him. "Just inform him ASAP."

We took off a few hours before dusk. My plan was to take a few pictures to substantiate my thesis and our findings, if there were any. I would move in after dark and lay up someplace close, overlooking the farm place and map it. Henry and I could keep in touch via the portables.

I grabbed the necessary baloney sandwiches that I made up from Henry's fridge, two cans of root beer, the only soda Henry drank, and packed everything into one of his old backpacks that read County Sheriff's Department on its flap in bright, florescent yellow.

Henry also gave me his extra police flashlight. He offered up his old camera, but I showed him my cell phone. It took great pictures and I could talk on it also. I asked Henry for the sheriff's office telephone number and his, too, to contact them. I speed-dialed them into my cell. However, both were out of my region and it was virtually just a camera that needed a computer to make it work. Or, if I connected, I'd have to pay exorbitant prices per minute for a call.

"Boy, you sure are making me feel out of step in this new-fangled electronic world. Although I'm feeling good at the same time remembering back in my day. That's the only camera I ever needed as sheriff. I wonder if I can still use it," Henry explained, looking it over. "Heck, there's still Kodak 120 film in it and several pictures got took and left on it. Wonder what they were," he mused, while looking up at the kitchen ceiling and into the past to remember...he couldn't.

"Henry, I respect you, I really do, but you can't go traipsing through that brush and along that creek at your age. Nevertheless, we can use portable radios to communicate with each other and I'll do it. I know what to avoid, I'm not sure what to look for, especially those people, since I only saw an old haggardly-looking woman with straight white hair. She must have been your age. There were others, but they snuck up behind me so quickly and threw whatever it was over me, I don't remember any faces."

"Well, as I recall, the old sheriff's sister would be ten, fifteen years younger than me. His ma would be in her nineties, so she'd probably be dead by now. Did you get a good look at that missing boy and girl flyer on the wall at the office…the Brandson boy and his girlfriend Sarah Tibbs?"

"Yes, you ran them off on the copier for me. I have those in my wallet, remember?"

"Ohhhh! I'm too darn old to be any good to anybody with a memory like mine!" Henry spoke out angrily showing his remorse.

"Don't peter-out on me now, old man," I said, just to incite his ire and arouse his courage to complete this job.

"Why, you little whippersnapper, I was bustin' big criminals long before you were just a smile on your daddy's face!" he barked.

I was successful. Henry would be in it for the long haul.

"Well, sheriff, what's your plan?" I asked Henry, to make him feel much needed. He seemed to regain his integrity and he put his hand upon my shoulder.

"Do you think that old gal is one of the old sheriff's relatives?" I asked.

"It might be one, or it might be one of the sisters' sisters or their kids. They were all a clan, remember? I think they were in-breeds. I was a fool not to do this while I was sheriff, but that's then, and I didn't think of it. That little girl would be his niece," he repeated. "I've got it! Her name was Nelly Hooley. She was illegitimate…I remember… talk of the town. That's why Judd took her mother in when he got the farm."

"Now who in the heck is this Judd?" I asked very confused.

"Why he was one of the elders in the church…he owns the farm we are headed to. I guess he still does…but, you know, I haven't talked to him since…since the Sunday before that massacre. Hummm."

"You mean it's been that long and you haven't been out to see him?"

"Oh, he was a rather funny-like fruitcake. He never took a shine to me. I steered clear of him. He'd get too close, if you know what I mean."

The rusty wheels were turning in old Henry's noggin and that was good. He was remembering more with every flashback. Except, he forgot to remember to tell me before I took off about the mean bulls

Judd raised in his pasture that he sold to someplace in Mexico for bull fighting.

"Testing, testing…can you hear me, Brad?"

"Yes, but you scared the heck out of me. I was crossing a barbed wire fence and now I'm stuck. Someone or something is moving around out there. I have to turn this thing off…catch ya later…bye!" I told him, to avoid being heard by someone, because of his blaring radio transmissions.

I had found a good place to cross the creek where Henry had pointed out that he "recollected" the footprints he saw back then were leading him. It had to be two or more miles to that farm, so it was going to certainly be an all nighter through the bramble and woods.

I took my time being as quiet as I could. I heard footsteps and shined my flashlight ahead. I saw three raccoons scrambling through the leaves, up to an old hollow tree. When I raised my flashlight they stopped and stood on their hind legs like real people; their eyes shown iridescently, just as I had seen deer in my headlights. The coons just watched me pass by, as I had entered an easier going through the woods. I looked up, and by gosh a full moon was rising. It seemed almost like daylight an hour later, but the going was slower than I could have imagined.

I walked across several fields I thought were what farmers called CRP. They were cleared, untilled, and weeds were left to grow tall there. I rustled up some deer in front of me that were sleeping in one field. When one of them snorted out like a real beast, I took off running so fast I ran into an old board fence gate and did a flip-flop right onto my keister. I wasn't hurt, just my pride.

Then I heard that deer blow out his air snorting again and they all began scampering away. I was letting the night get to me. Except, it was that reoccurring vision of that old woman that kept creeping into my thoughts. When I realized I was spooking myself, I thought surely I couldn't be harmed by an old lady, maybe with that cleaver though. I remained alert, but lost my direction.

I covered up my radio and turned it way down to call Henry. I thought if he honked his horn once, I could regain my direction.

"Henry…Henry! If you can hear me, honk your horn once, so I can get my bearings."

I listened, then I heard a honk. It was only a hundred feet away and I jumped higher than a yardstick. I had walked myself into a big circle. I bumped into a stump and sat down confused and forlorn. I began to itch and soon ants had crawled up my pants legs and under my sleeves…everywhere! I must have sat down on their hotel, because they were mad, biting and all over me like I was a jelly bread sandwich.

There was nothing I could do but disrobe and shake them off. I took off everything and danced around like a nut shaking off the ants. I'm glad no one saw me…well almost no one.

When I heard another snort, I assumed it was another deer I'd angered from its sleep. I should have listened better, then I would have heard those charging hooves headed my way. When I heard him next, I saw him, too, and when I saw him, too, I felt him, all at the same time.

A young, fierce, fighting bull had charged me and butted me with his small-ish horns. He was in the pasture and I was his practice dummy. He hit me solid and knocked me down and then pinned me and began to rub me into the ground.

Luckily, I shoved that backpack over his head and he couldn't shake it loose, until I had found the fence and leaped completely over it in the moonlight. There went my food and Henry's bag. But, I was amazed how I was able to do that…it was five feet tall. Of course, I was naked and lighter then. My clothes had gotten trampled upon, but not too badly.

After a few exhilarating, but futile attempts, with snorts and high kicks, that young bull finally shook off my backpack. He couldn't see me anymore and just wildly whirled around a few times; then he went prancing off like the king of the pasture.

I scurried to grab up my clothes and Henry's backpack. The food was gone. I returned to crouch near a big tree and put my clothes back on. But I had to flick off a few more remaining biting ants and then I put my clothes back on again. I planned to remain there, until nearing daylight.

The air smelled like I was near a dead rotting animal, so I moved farther away. I stayed away from old tree stumps and there looked like there were plenty. I just couldn't get away from that smell.

This was certainly not going well, I told Henry over the radio. I got no response after several loud attempts…moreover, I thought tired old Henry wasn't missing his needed nighttime sleep. I guess he just couldn't keep his eyes open. I looked at my watch and it was only ten. I decided to continue.

An hour later, or so, I saw lights. They appeared to be coming off pole lights in a distance, but they flickered on and off sometimes, emitting through the forest limbs. I knew they were shining from that farm.

The sky was full of stars and there was an occasional coyote howl and my imagination ran wild. I began enjoying myself not being afraid. I got downright brave. I guess it's what you can't see that causes fear.

Nearing dawn, it got lighter and I could see really well then without my flashlight. I now was making good time. I could also see there was just one little scrawny black bull running by his lonesome, but he now didn't want any part of me.

But there sure were a lot of dead carcasses scattered about, just as if they were butchered right there on the spot some time ago. Now they were fertilizer. That was the smell I couldn't get away from, no matter which way I walked.

When I had to wade another small creek, I stopped long enough to wash all over and drown those darn ants that just kept hanging in there. It was cooling and refreshing. Those ants really bit me all over. My face even felt itchy and sore. I must have looked like a badly diseased person.

At the dawning, my radio crackled and I heard Henry ask, "Brad, what the hell are you doing, son? Are you all right?"

"Good morning, sheriff! I'm slow, but I'm almost there. I'll contact you later. Why don't you take a snooze?" I suggested.

There was no reply, so I turned off my radio to save its battery. I looked around and saw the highest peak near the farm. It was in a wooded area so I headed over that way.

I couldn't believe how lucky I was when I spotted a hunter's deer stand high up in a tree and thought what a wonderful opportunity. It wasn't deer season, so I would be hidden and go unnoticed. I crawled up and sat on the seat. It was perfect…I could see everywhere, including the upstairs of the house and barn.

The house was a tall two story with a steeple-like top that looked like it might have been a church. It had lightning rods and pulled down window shades in all the windows except one, which was near the screened-in front porch. I looked for my car, but it was nowhere. That made me very angry.

There were six old dilapidated buildings, two concrete silos and one huge barn made of cinder brick and wood, all surrounded by tall weeds. The tinned, rusty-red roof was in need of repairs as many pigeons flew in and out. Some birds lined themselves for grooming at another shed's peak. I saw no people, but it was early. I saw fresh blood on the floor of the stand, so someone still used it out of season. Maybe they shot squirrels here, I imagined.

I wrote all this down in my notepad after I snapped off the cell phone pictures. If I had outside roaming on the cell, I could have just sent those pictures directly to the sheriff. I still had them stored up for when I got back to a computer for my eventual thesis.

Hours had passed and I had seen no one. I radioed Henry, but there was no answer. However, I imagined, if he could hear me clearly, he could understand that I told him I was five hundred feet from the farmhouse in a deer stand. He could then tell the sheriff that he had been contacted, just as I was ordered to keep him informed.

"Ten four?" I asked with no answer. Then I turned the radio off again. I felt I was getting nowhere.

I decided to get down and search around by the old barn. It was one time in my life that I wished I had stayed put and someone else had discovered what I came upon. The weeds in the old hog pen were tall, taller than I was, as I made my way to the farthest part of the farmyard and came back up behind the barn.

It was eerie, as good tractors stood in places, unprotected from the weather, as if someone had just stopped for lunch and never came back.

The shed was full of good machinery, too, but the dust on them was profoundly untouched, as I rubbed my hand across a small blue and gray Ford tractor's gas tank. It looked nearly new underneath the dust. I wondered why would someone just leave their good farm equipment out like that?

Then I saw something that really shook me. In the corner of the shed sat a clothed skeleton of a woman. Her wrists had been tied to the corner post and her head had rotted off her neck and had fallen onto her lap.

I had to breathe deeply, then try to hold my breath, while snapping off several pictures with my cell. When I got closer and a good whiff of the dead body stench, I looked for a place to hurl, but just let go. Then I heard voices.

I backed out of the shed and met a real surprise. Two barefoot men in bib overalls stood in my way with pitch forks pointed at me and took turns trying to make a shish kabob of me. It was early and maybe they were mad I had woke them. I ran back into the shed and I heard the door swing closed and the bar lock slam across the door.

One yelled out, "That's cornered him! Get Ma!"

I was desperate. I crawled upon my belly, up onto a tractor's tire and vaulted right through a side window that was missing panes. I tumbled into those tall weeds and saw two heads peek around the corner looking surprised at me. They came at me again prodding their forks wildly along the shed wall.

I picked up a flat rock and hurled it at the first man and hit him smack in the forehead. He squealed out like a stuck pig and the other screamed out towards the house for more help. Ten or fifteen small children came running from the house and stood there grouped up aimlessly, watching from the dusty road.

Then, that old white-haired freaky woman came off the screened-in porch steps waddling, and carrying a double barreled shotgun. When she saw me, she leveled those barrels my way and fired; luckily, she fired right after I had ducked to the ground. Fortunately, for me she missed.

Unfortunately, for one man who stood in front of me, he caught some stray buckshot and fell rolling around on the ground next to the other I hit with the rock. He began cussing his ma for what she did to him.

Blood immediately oozed through his bibs showing he got hit right in the belly. If it wasn't a mortal wound, he'd wish it was, without a doctor's help. He kept rolling around, squirming, and cussing his ma.

When I saw her reloading that shotgun from her apron's pocket, I turned and ran through those tall weeds and lay down again. Another blast cut weeds off much too near me, so I picked up a rock and threw it completely over the shed to the other side to distract her. She fired over that way, too. It worked, so I kept still, watching her search for any sight of me over there.

The old lady went to the children, hollering, screaming and then herded them back inside. They all wore the same bonnets with blue dresses, even though some apparently were boys. She returned to the yard and again began looking for me.

She waddled over to a large bell that was mounted on top of a pole and began pulling on a cord, which rang it continuously. I guess it had once been a farmer's dinner bell, for the wife to call in her husband from the fields. It was doing more than that now.

That was when I took more cell pictures of her, because she was still looking on the other side of the shed, where I had thrown the rock to fool her. Suddenly bursting out from the woods nearby came several armed men, who were running to the call of the bell.

When I thought I was surrounded with no escape route, I saw one bright flash that drew my attention. It was the gleam off my car's bumper. It had been pushed there most likely, because I had the keys and the spare key in my wallet. I had to make the break or get gunned down where I hid.

I crawled up a dry creek bed and behind the garage to my car. My intentions were to drive right out through the crowd with everything my engine had.

The shed was a tight fit, as I quietly eased along the interior wall, also too tight to open any door. I broke my own car window and slithered inside. Boy, was I surprised when there was no steering wheel, one fender was missing, my glove box was pried open and there was no front bucket seats to sit upon. Someone had striped the car and sold parts off it. My '69 Camaro was worth more together. It was my prize possession. Whoever did this didn't know diddly squat about classic cars, I thought, and that someone had just put his gun to my head.

CHAPTER FOUR

"Oops!" I said, rather hopefully that I'd still be alive on my next breath.

I was jerked out of the car door through the other side, which was apparently wider, then thrown down hard on the ground, and kicked senseless. After the first ten or twelve painful stomps, I didn't feel anything anyway.

I woke up feeling severe pain everywhere and sitting in a chair. My hands and feet were bound tightly with ropes that were cutting off circulation. There was a hood over my head that smelled like hair tonic from a barber shop. I guess it was a pillowcase.

I began to feel there were others in my presence. I heard shallow breathing and also snoring. I heard chairs creak from someone shifting his weight and that putrid smell of human decay again. I expected a bullet in my head at any moment and started to pray.

"Psssst!" someone hissed, trying to get someone's attention.

"Pssssst!" again sounded out.

"Psssssssssst, yourself," I half-consciously spoke to the irritating sound, which generated hurt inside my pounding brain.

"Psssst! If you can hear me, play dead and then they'll leave you alone. Keep that pillowcase over your head, because it's not good out here."

"I hear you, but do you have a hood on also?" I asked her.

"No, the last time they came in, the crud just left it off. I can't cry or scream anymore...I'm cried out and looking all around me, I wish I were dead, too. They killed my boyfriend, left him bleed to death right next to me and there's others here that look like they got chopped up..." she went silent.

I heard footsteps coming up a stairs, then stop for a moment and go back down.

"Pssst! Good, just let your head hang like that. You must have bad cuts on your head, you're bleeding badly. Maybe you'll get lucky and die."

Now I heard those words clearly and they registered. I wasn't going down without a fight.

"Who are you...Sarah Tibbs?"

"How did you know?"

"I'm helping the sheriff look for you. Eventually, if they don't kill us both first, he'll come in and get us. Hello? Hey?"

No one answered, so I hung my head again like I was dead, thinking someone else was watching me.

"Pssst! One of the kids saw you move and me, too. I think she went to tell them. Oh, God, help us now!"

Minutes passed, but no one came back upstairs. That child must have told them I was unconscious or had died. We waited and waited, until we heard arguing like I never heard it before. It seems old Ma didn't want anyone to come looking for me, so I was to be killed and buried with the rest.

"Jake! You and Charles go up there and take him out, kill him good, and bury him. Check his pockets for things to trade off at Coxiville. Watches are good, but rings bring more. Don't miss anything, we're low on everything. We'll have to eat some of them up there before winter, but that male up there will be too tough, cause he fought so hard before he died...heathen male testosterone toughens and spoils the meaty taste," she ordered them. "Bury your brothers out by the shed, too, on your way out. Darvin caught one of my strays in his gut. He's hurtin' bad and needs to be saved from too much hurtin'. Do him in when he's not lookin'. He was such a good boy."

"No! Do it yourself. I did all the dirty work last time. I like that girl up there and I want her for my own. If I get her, then I kill that male and that's that," he quarreled.

"Oh, no, sireee, you don't! She be mine! All mine!" yelled one at the other.

Then the darnest ruckus fighting began. Chairs were turned over and it sounded as if a utensil drawer had been pulled out and its contents hit the floor. There were grunts and howls of pain and lots of cussing.

We could hear one dare the other to go ahead and stab him, because he was gutless, and that's evidently what he did. There was a terrible moan of pain. I heard the muffled thud that sounded as if a butcher had stuck his knife in a beef. Then he moaned more loudly and fell to the floor.

"You dirty…" and then his words halted.

"See what you did! Kilt your own brother over some weird gal. Now, you go bury him, your brothers, too, and come back and destroy them upstairs. If you don't I'll blow your head off…hear me now…I'm a'tellin' ya…get!"

I don't know how that girl survived, but I knew the end was near. I began chewing the hood, until it filled my mouth and I jerked up and down, inching it off, until I could peek out. It was horrifying and I froze in fear from the appalling sight. I almost lost it all there.

Sara Tibbs looked ghastly, also. She still wore her prom dress, but it was blood-splattered and she looked like a zombie. Her body looked very frail and emaciated, because she starved herself, refusing to eat the human flesh brought to her.

What vicious animals had that much abhorrence in them to slay the masses who were laying sprawled out, sectioned, some dismembered for its meatier hunks. On the far wall some were heaped up, stacked on top of each other; must have been nearly fifty pieces. Then I saw the ones who appeared gutted, skinned and salted, hanging by their loins from rafters to cure like a ham. There appeared to be smoked human sausages hanging from strings, too.

When I heard the screen door from downstairs slam, my adrenaline must have peeked. It was now or never before they returned to butcher me.

I stood up, then sat down hard and crashed the chair to the floor. It broke apart, but the ropes remained secure. I rolled around and desperately tried to get untied. I was making too much noise.

Then I heard one person's steps quickly coming up the stairs, so with all that I had, I managed to stand up. I hopped over to the open stairwell and saw the tip of a huge knife blade first. I was still tied up, no time to think, so I bailed out into the air and dropped down hard on top of him. We crashed into his ma, who had waddled up behind him with her shotgun.

We all came down hard on the floor, but the old woman must have broken her back, I think. When she landed with a big thump, she came down upon the kitchen table leg's footrest. She screeched out a horrible moan.

Nevertheless, the man held tight to his dagger, rolled over and came up looking at me. I kicked chairs and anything I could to get away, still trying to free myself. He stalked me like a freakish fiend with blood in his eyes.

I kicked and clawed my way around that table again and again to get away from his lunges, until finally, I caught the man's groin with a very swift kick. When he momentarily folded over, I jumped on his head and he hit the floor hard facedown. I stomped him several times, until he did not move.

While he lay motionless, I grabbed up his long butcher knife from the floor and stabbed him the only place my tied arms allowed…in his throat. He woke up then, screaming and kicking, holding his pain. I backed up watching the life squirt out of him and hacked at the rope around my knees, so I could stand with my legs apart.

Then I whacked at my wrists and cut myself, because I did not have the angle to cut. The old lady still lay facedown on the bloody floor, but she was breathing.

"Are you still all right up there?" I hollered out to Sarah.

"I'm still here!" she yelled back. "What the heck happened down there? It felt as if the whole house shook."

I then worked on my ropes, until I reached my cell in my pants pocket. I dropped it twice, until I laid it on the bloody kitchen table and punched keys with one finger that wasn't bloody. I got lights, but the signal was weak. Suddenly, I got a full red line and dialed up 911. I bent my ear down next to the cell to hear it, just as I got one hand slipped free.

"Monroe County Sheriff's. What is your emergency?"

"This is Deputy Brad Anderson…tell the sheriff to get out here fast!" I yelled, just as another man dashed inside and attacked me.

I dropped the cell and defended myself; my life depended upon it. I hit him with my fist, but that just knocked him down. He was getting up and pulled out a long slender pocket knife. The look in his eyes, his mad face, was of a maniac, just like the others.

I whacked him with a chair leg across his extended arm and he dropped the knife on the floor, long enough for me to bolt away. But he still grabbed onto me and we wrestled.

I had spotted the double barreled shotgun laying on the floor behind the kitchen door and worked my wrestling moves over towards it. I quickly grabbed the gun, pointed at his head and hoped it was loaded. His eyes grew wide and he was scared to death then and backed up.

"Click, click!" He wasn't scared of me anymore.

The gun was empty, so when he came all-out at me, I used it as a club. When the butt of that gun hit the jaw of the advancing maniac, he dropped like a ton of bricks. I could see I broke his jaw. But I looked for another attacker when I heard a noise.

I saw my reflection in a very cloudy bedroom dresser's mirror and took guard. Then I realized that bloody figure was me. I picked up my cell.

"Hello! Hello!"

"Brad, the sheriff says hold on…he'll be there quickly. Do you need an ambulance? Is Henry there with you?"

"I think so, yes, yes! There must be a hundred people dead up here. Oh, my God! I found the Tibbs girl alive, but I think her boyfriend, Tom Brandson has been dead a week. Oh, my God!" was all I could say before I began to have a severe comprehension problem and headache. The more I moved around, the more it seemed to help. When I stood still, I almost would collapse.

When I heard more noises, I searched the cabinets for more shotgun shells and found several in a Winchester box. I loaded up, put more in my pocket and went upstairs. I was surprised to see several persons looking up at me and others still moving. They had pretended to be dead as Sarah had told me to do.

I went to the kidnapped girl, Sarah, first and after I untied her she fell down next to her boyfriend and began bawling loudly. Then I heard sirens and went back downstairs with the shotgun.

The sheriff was hitting every pothole and his car was bouncing all over the road. I turned on my portable and told him to slow down. I called Henry several times, but he didn't answer. I was so bloody, the sheriff did not even know me. He had drawn his gun on me and told me, "Put up your hands and drop that shotgun."

I guess I had used up my full charge. Suddenly, like a flashlight battery going dead, I just passed out in front of him. The next thing I knew, I had a wrap on my head, an oxygen attachment in my nose and a cold cloth washing my face. I was being shaken hard by the ambulance swaying to and fro, while headed for the hospital. I heard the EMT tell the dispatcher to call in the state police and every ambulance they could muster. There were bodies everywhere. I returned to unconsciousness.

When the sheriff arrived at my hospital bed, I was surprised it was so quickly. He asked me immediately what had happened to Henry.

"Henry? Henry...oh...I think I talked to him on the radio...I can't remember when though. I can't remember anything. Where am I?"

"Sorry, sheriff, this man is in a severe condition and it could deteriorate into shock. He lost a lot of blood and probably will not come around for a while, because I have to put him under again, until the brain swelling is relieved...hopefully, I won't have to go inside."

"What's all wrong with him, Doc?"

"Sheriff, it's as though he was in a really bad wreck. I put over three dozen stitches in him from his head, on down to his feet. X-ray showed a large subdural pressure formed by clotting in his brain from a direct blow or two in the head," he spoke.

The doctor said I was out for quite a while and had received a concussion and internal bleeding. He had just revived me back into consciousness, however ten days had passed. It was longer than I realized, but I knew who he was.

Slowly, I began to remember, but I was still on medication and not really coherent yet. The sheriff came in again and started asking questions, which my slow mind had trouble comprehending without deep thought.

"Brad, this is important. The world is outside wanting to know about your horrible discovery. There's more news people out there than I've ever seen in my entire life and I don't have their answers. Do you remember anything?"

"Sure, everything, why?"

After the doctor told me I had been unconscious ten days, he said some things had occurred that I was totally unaware. That set me back. It seemed as if I just napped for a moment.

"We finally found Henry," the sheriff began.

"Was he sleeping? I tried to get him on the portable when I was shot at by that white haired person...but he quit answering. Henry sure is a friendly person though. Maybe he went to check on his camera film," I spoke, still in delirium.

"We buried him yesterday, Brad. We found him, his throat was slit and his car pushed off the road up against a tree...off that entrance road. Might have been there a day, we aren't certain yet. Can you tell us everything you can and speak into this recorder?" the sheriff asked.

"Oh, I have my cell pictures, too. I took as many as I could. I can't...What! Henry is dead?" it suddenly dawned on me what was being said. "May God rest his soul...he was my friend...I'm sorry...that I brought all this on with my investigation. You buried him already? He wanted to see what was on his old camera at his home...it might have been something important to him, he thought. He didn't remember too well. I didn't even get to say good-bye," I rambled.

"Okay, Brad...now tell me everything from the beginning. This might be the biggest case you and I will ever work on. Ready? I need your statement," he said, turning on his recorder.

It took four long hours, breakfast, and several cups of coffee to tell my tale. It wasn't a tale per se, it was my conclusion of a really horrendous nightmare, not only for me, but the twenty people or so, including the children who survived the assault. I had killed three or four in self defense.

Margaret "Ma" Parker, her seven nephews, Wilbur, Jake, Bartholomew, Charles, Alphonse, Carl and Darvin and her one illegitimate daughter named Ellie were all accounted for, either dead or alive.

Three other men were apprehended alive, somehow related to the clan. Thirty unknown souls had been discovered by canine cadaver dogs alerting on their separate grave sites throughout the property, so far, the sheriff related.

"What about those boy scouts. Did you recover any of them?"

"Unbelievably, the Hooley clan people were all cannibalistic. We think they were eaten by the family, soon after they were attacked. We found juvenile bones in one grave.

"Margaret Parker was a then newly-released mental case from the state facility in Alton. Of course, DNA will match with the boys' relatives, but will take some time as they uncover more of the mass graves. There's sixty forensics working out there now...it's like a gigantic morgue and archeological study going on at the same time out there right now."

"Oh, my God! What about that girl who helped me...ah...Sarah Tibbs?"

"She's here in the hospital. She's having a terrible time and her injuries are deep in her mind, not on her body. You might see her."

"I want to."

I asked the sheriff for a copy of my statement and he said it would be made. He was certain any arrests for the culprits caught alive would never go to court because they were all obviously insane.

In about a week, my parents came to see me from Florida. I had called them as soon as I was stable enough to tell them I was fine and recouping. We visited, but I wasn't able to tell them I had to kill humans. They stayed for only a few hours, but left to visit other relatives when they knew I was fine. I think it was very hard on them, too, because they had seen the TV reports and read the newspapers, also.

When the doctor came in to tell me I was scheduled to be released, he asked me if I would visit Sarah Tibbs. She had been brought to my floor and needed mental support. I dressed and went to her room.

"Hi, Sarah...remember me, Brad...you saved my life," I spoke to her softly.

"You look different without that hood and blood all over you... but I remember your kind voice. Thank you for saving the rest of us," Sarah spoke.

"Sarah, when you get released, and you will, I want to take you out to dinner, okay?"

My journalistic mind thought about an exclusive from her was a story on its own. We talked, but I could see she was still not free from her torment. Only time could heal us all.

I finally met with the media throng and gave my statement along side the sheriff. He later asked me to become a full fledged deputy, but I had that thesis to write and fall college classes were nearing and I hadn't begun.

I worked diligently, after meeting and getting an extension from my professor on finishing my thesis. After six months of piecing as much together as I could, I began wondering about the final outcome.

I received a commendation by mail, when I refused to accept it in person. I had to forget, not regenerate those horrible thoughts again. Enclosed in the envelope was a statement from the forensic authorities and their simple resulting statement.

"On June 03, 1956 a family of insane cannibalistic humans named Hooley attacked and kidnapped sleeping Boy Scout campers in their tents. They also slayed four adult chaperones. The captured nine boys were held hostage; eventually the cannibals ate the boys, over a period of three years. A fifty-two year investigation has been closed."

CHAPTER FIVE

That wasn't good enough for me. A first-rate journalist always searches for the "why". I went back to the small town and searched for anyone who could recall the days of 1953.

I stopped in a local tavern and sat upon a stool nursing a Ski soda and hoping someone would become friendly enough to talk to me. The bartender was middle-aged and seemed set on washing the glasses and sweeping the floor for the night crowd that came in after work and those softball players whose team he sponsored.

It was cool and comfortable and I felt my ninety mile drive up from Carbondale was about to be fruitless, until I noticed a peculiar string that ran along the ceiling and to a tiny bell. It was tinkling.

"Sir!" I spoke to the bartender, as he stooped down and swept up the dust into his dustpan. He looked up, didn't say a word, dumped the dust, then he casually came over to me.

"Ready for another Ski, or you want a big boy's drink now? It's after three," he chimed smiling.

"Yes, another Ski, but can I ask why the bell?"

"Mom! She needs her TV channel changed."

"Why don't you just get her a remote?" I said, and thought would simplify the situation.

"She's too old. I put on her favorite channels, but now she watches the soaps and she watches channel five. I'm surprised she can see that well for ninety-eight years come October."

My instincts just told me to offer up my services to change Mom's channel for her, just as three businessmen-looking customers strolled in for "Something cold!" one wanted.

The bartender looked at his customers and then the ringing bell sounding again.

"Say, I'd be glad to go up and change Mom's channel for her. Does she like 'As the World Turns,' also? I do, too!"

"You're kidding, right? Okay, thanks, go knock yourself out, but be nice to Momma Tillie!"

I didn't need another invitation, so I headed to the backroom and up the narrow staircase to the upper rooms. I walked to the sounds and there she was. She raised her cane from her chair as if she thought I was a robber.

"Now, sonny, I ain't got nothin' you'd want, but could you change the channel to…"

"To… 'As the World Turns'," I broke in… "my favorite…mind if I watch with you?"

I took the remote off the adjacent coffee table and changed the channel, just as the first scene began. The lady just kept one eye on me and one on the program for several moments.

"Where is my boy, Johnny?" she asked.

"Your loving son is overrun with customers and has asked me to come up here to help his lovely mother."

"You're so full of bull crap…you forgot to say 'old' mother," she chuckled. "Quiet! This is where he gets his!" she squealed and shook her cane at the TV with excitement.

I thought there would be a shooting, but instead, it was a romantic bedroom scene. I laughed at her intense enjoyment of the lovers kissing.

"Darn commercials…can't never see the good parts," she complained.

I sat there wondering how to approach her about the infamous "Hootenanny Massacres".

I just waited for the end and she said, "Channel four news!"

I changed it to four. It was another murder report from East St. Louis that they were talking about and she was disinterested, showing disgust on her face.

"Mom…may I call you Mom?"

"Well I certainly hope so…all my customers used to call me mom, back then," she advised.

"Back when?" I questioned.

"When I owned the tavern and there really were customers that kept me busy. Johnny just doesn't have what it takes…he's all business and no gab. You have to mingle with your friends, they're not just your customers. Why I had a house full of friends every night after the factories let loose."

"What factories?"

"Chrysler, Ford, Chevrolet…all the manufacturing car plants were in St. Louis. The guys would team up and buy vans, so then ten or twelve could go back and forth to work together to save gas. Some slept, while one drove each week. I always gave the driver a free tab that week to get him to stop in after work. After a while, they all knew me as Mom."

"How long did you barkeep?"

"Aren't you listenin', sonny? I invited them into my home, my home, not my tavern."

"Sure, I understand, but how long?"

"Since…ah…the fall of forty-four, when the big war was over."

"So, you were around when the Hootenanny Massacres happened, huh?"

"Right in the middle. I donated to those poor kids. I gave them what I could. They were all my good children…especially all of them boys…I knew them all…fathers and the preacher."

"Would you tell me about what happened?"

"You're a reporter, ain't ya? I figured so. You ask too many questions."

"Not yet, but I want to be. My name is Brad Anderson and I'm a college student trying to become a journalist. I was assign…"

"You're that kid that broke it wide open, ain't ya! I recognize ya now off channel four news!" she interrupted.

"I guess so. But this place is twenty or so miles from the farm place and Coxiville is even farther. Why did they come here?"

"You still ain't listenin'! I had friends…lots and lots of friends. When someone was broke and down on their luck, I gave 'em what I could to get them back on their feet. They always repaid…cause I was

Mom and their best friend. They come from all the surroundin' towns to stop by.

"I had little league ball teams, men's softball, women, too, for a while…had bowling teams, boys, girls, men and women all at Paultler Heights…and the best euchre teams goin' of all time. My pool league was good, too. I gave all my children fun and they in turn came here when they needed Mom. I'm hungry, are you, too?" she suddenly asked me.

"Yes, can I get you something?"

"Can you make a good burger?"

"It depends…what you call a 'good burger'."

"Go down stairs to the freezer and get some of them froze-up burgers…and fire up the grill, if it ain't already. I like mine near raw with the buns left on top of the grill with the grease. Doctor says, "No", but I'm ninety- ah…ninety something, so I can eat what I want."

I met Johnny coming up the stairs to check on his mom and I told him she just asked me to make her a burger.

"Okay, thanks…I'm glad for your help. Need a poor paying job?" he laughed out.

"No, but I'm enjoying the visit with Mom."

"Oh, she's told you how great this place was back in the day, right?"

"Yes, and I'm very pleased to learn all about that…"

"Hey…you're that guy who found all those bodies out at Judd Parker's farm. Saw you on the tube…glad to meet you. You were in a mess, huh? You brought in a lot of customers for me, for a few months to watch the news and talk about whose relatives were being found… your lunch today, sir, is on me…if you make Mom's, too, ha!"

Johnny told me to make myself at home, everything was in his big freezer. I realized he was getting his mother's trusting attitude.

I went to cooking and I prepared those hamburgers. The burgers were pre-made from the freezer, and conveniently wrapped in waxed paper. I threw three fat ones on the hot gill and the buns, too. I found a serving tray and when the burgers were almost half-done, I scooped them off and put them on the gooey-toasted buns and then onto paper plates. I found onions, pickles, mustard and ketchup and put it all on a separate plate. When I saw root beer, I also took two along upstairs. I was prepared to hear the whole real story.

When Mom took her false teeth out to rinse them in her root beer, I felt queasy, but nothing could stop me now after what I had been through. I waited for her to finish with a big hiccup from her long slug of root beer, then asked about the massacre.

"Mom, I could tell by the twinkle in your lovely blue eyes that you knew a lot about what happened out there. The case has been officially closed, because all the bodies have been accounted for, except the scouting party bones are being DNA'd and Judd Parker's is missing still."

"What's your name again?"

"I'm Brad Anderson."

"Okay, Bradley...you've been a good boy, so I'll give you the lowdown. Back in forty-four or forty-five, I began here as a helper to Judd Parker's mom and dad who were second generation farmers and owned this place to give them money to buy more land. Drinkin', gamblin' and partyin' was heavy with all the boys back home from the war and taverns were as good as gold mines back in those days.

"But when Margaret became pregnant with Judd, she quit comin' to work and I was offered her job, just till Judd was born. Now there came a ruckus as to whose father was Judd's, because Judd didn't look like either of his parents. Margaret loved that boy and bought him everything he wanted as her only child.

"In the meantime, I was making good tips, because all the boys thought I was pretty. I used to fight them off, Judd's daddy, Elmer, too.

"One night, Margaret caught Elmer bein' drunk and trying hard to corner me and kiss me. I was fighting him hard to keep my distance up. Margaret just up and shot Elmer dead. He didn't have a gun, but he always got that way with women when he was drunk at the end of the day, because of him accepting all his friends a'buyin' him drinks... he sure got stupid by quittin' time.

"Elmer was very popular amongst the crowds and some of them so-called friends got on the jury after the sheriff, Fess Border, arrested Margaret for murder and took her to jail.

"They say Fess offered her a deal to keep her mouth shut about him being Judd's real poppa. When Margaret was going to spill the beans, the sheriff up and had her committed to the nut house. Well, she wasn't nuts, until she spent twenty years in Alton around those others. She got that way in there.

"In all that meantime, I had bought this tavern from Judd, so he could pay off one of his dad's farms…and I ran it ever since. Old Elmer left a lot of cash. And it was all Judd's…Margaret nary got a cent.

"Judd got good at farmin', real good, but bein' an only child with a mother in the nut house caused him much pain in his schoolin'.

"Judd quit school at sixteen and went into full-time farmin'. He had bought up so much ground on credit, because the grain prices were really good and he was always known to work his hind end off. One by one, he owned more farms and got good men as his helping hands. Some say he made advances at his help.

"He never sought a woman. Then, he met Rebecca Begonia. She was a slut off the streets of St. Louis and hot to trot and everyone knew it. She saw Judd's money and wanted it any way she could get it. They got hitched and something happened again. Rebecca had babies, some were twins…a baby girl they named Ellie May, and her twin sister, Sophia May, that nobody but me ever knew about, cause Judd once told me at the tavern that Sophia was bornt water head. Rebecca birthed those two right out there in that farm house and they wasn't Judd's.

"About then, when money got short in the state capital, someone just set Margaret loose. Some say she found her way back to the farm right away and started scarin' off the help. I knew Judd had done went and got her cause he talked drunk again. They said Margaret right away started eating raw pork or anything else that was raw. She had a taste for blood and they just threw her raw meat like a dog at that place. That's what she learnt at that asylum. About then, too, the slut and her babies livin' there just went away and no one saw or heard of them since."

"Margaret Parker, right?"

"Margaret, or Ellie May. I never seen them since she shot Elmer. I suppose I must go to the police and tell them what I know. It is the only right thing to do before another baby disappears into the night."

"What do you mean, another baby?" I was shaken.

"Don't you watch the channel four news anymore? It's been on a month. Baby missin' near Waterloo. Mother left her in the stroller to go pick up milk down an aisle and when she turned around the baby was snatched up."

"Sophia did it?"

"I'm a'thinkin' that by the way it happened…it was her alright. She had this affliction like her mother. Judd would come, get drunk as a skunk, and start tellin' me tall tales of her chasin' and catchin' his chickens, a'ringin' their necks till their heads popped off, then drink the hot blood right out of the polt's neck, squirtin' red like a stream. She did it to his baby pigs, too…ate up all his chickens. He started feeding her raw meat to keep her from attackin' his high priced beef stock. He had fightin' bulls.

"Now, there's somethin' I can't be a'tellin' ya truthful, cause I don't know much. It's said that Judd got a girl pregnant in town and she had his baby, but I heard that across the bar, not from Judd his self.

"I figure I know where Sophia's a'hidin out now. They used to keep her penned up in a big false closet upstairs there, ever since she was bornt. No one's been a'feedin' her since the raid, I bet. She's come out for eats. She be blood thirsty…someone better find her.

"I have faint loyalty to her because Margaret shot Elmer over me, but she has grown into a mad person and I cannot stand the anxiety waiting to hear of her next deed. Yes, Sophia was the one left behind, they all thought dead, so I owed Margaret and Elmer that much due.

"Now evidently Sophia has become an old woman and her meals are no more. Her wits left her at birth; she has bats in her belfry.

"I alone know how she got that way. It was neither her fault nor mine. It was that odd Fess, and his son legit, Judd, who lived in that secluded Hooley farmhouse away from the town. Judd was self-contained there and never needed anything. He had all his farm animals, crops and garden vegetables for his table. He was never in need, including wanting the almighty dollar."

"Will you call the sheriff ,Tillie, or should I?" I asked.

"First change the channel to Jeopardy. You call," she ordered.

That afternoon the sheriff came to the tavern in Foster Pond and talked with the ninety-eight year old, while I took notes.

Tillie Schroeder thought she knew where Sophia Parker was and where she might be hiding. She spoke right out.

"Once, Judd came into this tavern and had hurt his thumb real bad and it was swollen. He was a'downin' whiskeys as fast as he could get them gulped down to kill the pain. After he got talkative-drunk, as always, he said he had built a secret bedroom for his Sophia above the kitchen. He rigged it above the sink, last cabinet door; there's a dropdown ladder. That's where he got his thumb caught and hurt in that hinge. Then once upon a time, he said it was too hot up there for his Sophia and he found a place near the creek, by the little one-lane horse bridge that crossed the creek behind the house. But, she started stalking his cattle and kilt and chewed up a few of his prize animals. She'd eat the little one's she could catch at nighttime."

The sheriff looked startled at me…"That's just where we found Henry," he told me.

"Henry? Henry who?" Tillie asked.

"Henry Holcombe, my deputy, he was murdered right near there. I thought maybe a coyote or wild dog got to him…he was out of his car on the ground…he looked gnawed upon."

"I knew Henry since he played on one of my teams. He married that Ellis girl from Hecker. She's been gone a while, but I last saw Henry when I voted for him as sheriff. That saddens me…he was a good boy," Tillie said with remorse. "Oh, if I hadn't been so dumb. Take me to jail!"

I guess if she had come forward much earlier, people's lives might have been saved. Tillie was never actually out there and had only Judd's hearsay about everything. But, now she had Henry on her conscience, too. I was glad to be privy to the inside information and hoped capturing Sophia would stop the carnage.

The sheriff surely wasn't going to arrest Tillie as an accomplice by withholding evidence. Before the time came that she would go to court she'd already be dead. It was hard to understand the real "why" Tillie hadn't come forward, but it was too late, I thought.

This was part of the final sheriff's report synopsis.

"Acting on Tillie Schroeder's information, the sheriff and his men re-searched the Parker home and found a secret fold-down ladder in the kitchen cabinet and climbed up there. They found an adult woman, unclothed, and in a state of mental derangement, who the sheriff believed to be Sophia Parker. She was saturated in blood stains.

"Apparently, she had lived in that room for all of her years and learned everything from her mother Rebecca. It is surmised by physical evidence that she must have helped devour Rebecca and Ellie, because their remains so indicated. However, numerous women's clothing of multiple sizes and fashion hung unscathed on hangers. Sophia might have dawned some of those clothes to enter town in disguise, but it is highly unlikely. She was so deranged, one must wonder how she could know where to go?

"A deceased, partially-eaten and recently abducted baby's remains were still there, also."

That was the summation. Again, I personally couldn't imagine how she got all the way into the store to kidnap the child from its own mother. She had to have help. The sheriff told me other information.

The long-dead, skeletal remains of Judd Parker sat clothed and undisturbed, propped up in a corner with other human bones. There were fresh dandelions picked from the overgrown yard grass from that very day and had been sprinkled upon his carcass.

Apparently, Sophia thought well of Judd, maybe he was her doll, father figure, or whatever a mentally ill person could contrive. Still, I couldn't conceive her as being the sole culprit.

CHAPTER SIX

It wasn't until I fell into a bit of luck again at the Monroe County Sheriff's auction that I discovered the final piece of the puzzle. I had heard from Sheriff Fischer. He told me that he was to sell off Henry's home and personal property for taxes. His two old hounds had been put down.

I thought of that Kodak camera of Henry's and how he reacted when he had found old pictures were still on there undeveloped. I was sort of curious myself of his sudden remorse for not developing them sooner.

"Sold! For twenty dollars!" the auctioneer rattled off, as he pointed to me. I purchased Henry's service revolver, too.

I decided to go by Wal-Mart to see if those Kodak 120 film pictures could still be developed. The clerk told me it would be better if I finished taking the next eight pictures that were left on the film, before I tried to remove it. That way they wouldn't be exposed to light.

I decided "what the hey" and took it along with me to the barbershop. I pulled up in front of the establishment and thought a picture of that whirling barber pole might be nice to see and might be obsolete some day. After I snapped one or two of the street and buildings, I found myself inside the shop about to get a trim with two pictures left.

"Smile, George," I said, looking at the barber and he at my camera. I took a last shot of him cutting someone's hair.

When it was my turn to get my haircut, I noticed this George was George S. Border on his barber's certificate. I thought maybe that was just a coincidence as I got my ears lowered. Later, I dropped off my film at Wal-Mart to be developed.

When I received those photos back a week later from Wal-Mart, my mouth dropped open. There was Sheriff Fess Border in his uniform, Ellie Parker and Rebecca Parker, and a very young George Border, my new barber, standing together in a picture. Henry had to have taken the picture. I then had a strong hunch, but I had to do some acting.

When I remembered I still had that sheriff's deputy badge in my wallet, I took the pictures to George and acted like I knew it all. I suspected now I knew Sophia's accomplice, probably the baby's kidnapper.

George was surprised that I was back so soon to get a haircut and he kept asking what was wrong with my last haircut. I just let him simmer, cutting another's hair, until he was finished and we were alone.

Then, I fumbled out my badge from my wallet and let it fall onto the floor. It bounced off the hardwood and then fell at his feet, which really caused George concern. I slowly picked it up, rising to look George straight in the eyes, but never said I was the law.

It was then I smelled that same fragrance from that pillowcase that had been used as a hood on me at the farm house. I was mad.

With my most stern face, I asked George straight out, "How were you related to Sophia Parker?" as I showed him the picture. When he froze stiff, I gave him my TV version of his Miranda warning starting with, "You have the right to remain silent"…he broke right then and there.

"Oh, my! Oh, my…you finally found out, didn't you?" he said, with some relief and a big gasp. "Well, I'm somewhat relieved…take me to jail…every time she does something like what she has, I die inside. Sophia is my niece, of course. Judd Parker was my half-brother, too, but he didn't claim me. He brought us food though, while I was young and until Mom passed he came by. He then sent me to barber school and paid for that. I don't hate him, but he never loved me like he loved Sophia and she him.

"I've been driving by the Parker farm road every night after work since the police raid and leaving food for Sophia in the old unpainted mailbox. She comes out in the night and eats it right there, then she crawls back up into that hole, that is until they found Ma. Did she tell you I sometimes helped her?"

"Did you help her kill all of the victims?"

"I better stop talking and call my lawyer," he said, then sounding very weak and suddenly very sissified. "May I close up shop?" he asked politely.

"Sure, George, you've been truthful with me. I'll tell you what…I trust you; you go ahead…drive to the sheriff's office and turn yourself in. That might help your case during the sentencing. You know, they need good barbers in the jail."

Old George wasn't smiling then. He was shivering and wobbly. But I thought I wasn't a real deputy then either; I thought I was just pretending.

At the time, also, I hoped I wasn't in trouble myself for impersonating a police officer. That's why technically, I didn't place him under arrest.

When George was about to leave on his own, I used his phone to call the sheriff and gave him my new information that George was enroute.

Sheriff Fischer wanted me to bring George in myself, but George was already on his way, I told him. I am a man of my word, so I let George turn himself in, as planned, but followed him to the door. He went inside and quickly confessed.

I later found out that day that I was still sworn in as a special deputy, just in case I was called into court to testify. It never went down that way. Consequently, when I went to George to interview him, I was officially a law enforcement officer and I was correct to have given him his Miranda rights, before I questioned him and he confessed guilt. Otherwise, everything I learned before that, I would not have been able to testify.

George Border was charged as an accessory to a homicide; which one, I was never certain. I suspected he was the one who took the baby.

George must have gotten a good attorney to plead guilty to just one victim to lessen his chance of a death sentence. Everyone else in that clan who was alive was ruled insane and incapable of knowing what they did was wrong. They all went to secure mental prison institutions, but George was ruled sane and could have been executed.

Why any people do wrong is strange to me. It's a selfish act, unless it is perpetrated to stay alive. In a short time, I had learned there are all kinds of reasons that trigger a criminal's mind, mostly greed and being too lazy to work for what they want. Prison may change their attitude to commit crimes as a deterrent; however, if they are insane they probably can not be rehabilitated, if returned to their same environment from which they came.

In September, I drove down to SIUC for my last year. College was busy and my detective journalist endeavor was brought up by my professors. After I completed my senior year, I put in an addendum to my thesis, right before I received my Bachelor of Arts degree, cum laude. I had graduated.

When my college studies were ended, I was then in need of a job. My planned occupation as a newspaper journalist seemed void of the kind of excitement I had experienced in the past year's police investigation, unless I was reporting directly from the current war zones in Afghanistan.

Consequently, I called the Monroe County Sheriff's office to talk to Sheriff Clyde Fischer, my new friend, about the final outcome of George Border. His trial surprisingly went quickly.

The sheriff told me that George Border was now scheduled to be cutting hair in Menard State Penitentiary in Chester, Illinois for a very long time.

Then the sheriff asked me to become his fulltime deputy. Monroe county was an up and growing region and it could be a place to begin a career, I thought. I applied, went to the police academy school in Springfield for three months, and then graduated with my certificate. I returned to Monroe County to receive full sheriff's deputy status.

I found my first real employment there, as I rode patrol in Monroe County. The sheriff had talked me into it, but also told me the air of adventure might never be as exciting again. I told him I hoped so; imagine that?